A Hood Chick's Story

Presented by

LaShonda DeVaughn

Editor: www.hightowereditorialservices.com

In Loving Memory of

Andre Stone

March 25, 1987 – September 18, 2005

Knock! Knock! Knock!

I heard an obnoxious banging on my apartment door. It seemed as if the door was about to cave in. I opened the door only to find my cousin Tamika in tears. I could barely understand what she was saying.

"Girl come in, what's wrong?"

"T, it's Derek!"

I tried to calm her down, "What do you mean it's Derek?"

"He just got shot!" Tamika cried.

I felt my head spin. "Who told you this? Are you sure it's Derek, *my* Derek?"

"Yes Tiara, *your* Derek," she insisted. "He was rushed to the hospital and it ain't looking good T."I began sobbing uncontrollably; all I could do was drop to my knees and pray. It couldn't be Derek, not my first love. I had just talked to him an hour ago!

It was Christmas Eve and he told me he was going

1

to the mall to shop for last minute gifts. I just knew that my prayers would change the news that Tamika had just told me. My mom came in when she heard us crying and tried to calm us down. She kept saying how there must've been some sort of mistake, but there wasn't.

It was crazy like that in the hood.

I'll get back to Tamika and Derek in a minute but first let me introduce myself and tell you how it all started.

My name is Tiara James, but my friends call me T. I'm your around the way don't take no shit from no one type of girl. My slanted eyes, butterscotch golden complexion, shoulder length hair and hour glass shape has coined me the label "a dime piece."

I grew up in the streets of Boston, Massachusetts also known as "The Bloody Bean." People seemed to think that Boston was full of good colleges and minimal hoods, that's not the case at all. New York has its five boroughs: Manhattan, Queens, Brooklyn, Bronx and Staten Island. Boston has four; Dorchester, Mattapan, Roxbury and South End. I grew up in Dorchester, borderline Mattapan also known as "Murderpan."

It was like any other hood. Violence, robbing and killing ran the streets. And either you ran with it or you ran from it. Growing up, I tried to observe everything and rise above it but sometimes you just fall victim to everything around you.

I was born in Norfolk Virginia and moved to Boston after my mom left and divorced my abusive, alcoholic father. My mom had two kids by my father, me and my brother Trè James. Trè and I witnessed my mother being abused countless times at the hand of our father. One time in particular my father was beating my mom with closed fists as if he was in a Mike Tyson fight. He was on top of her punching her defenseless body, blow by blow to her chest and face.

Trè must've had so much anger built in him from witnessing all the other ass whippings that he went in the closet to get the bat that he used for baseball practice and showed his skills by knocking my father in the head.

I couldn't believe what I saw.

One blow to my father's head sent blood streaming down his face like a waterfall. My father managed to take the bat from Trè, but the guilt from hitting my mom caused him not to retaliate, instead he just left.

Later that night he came home drunk out of his mind.

His clothes smelled like he had taken a bath in Tequila and he could barely keep his balance.

My brother Trè and I were watching TV with my mom in her room when my father came in the room yelling and cussing.

"All y'all get the fuck out of here, I'm tired and I want to lie down!"

My mom hated when he cursed in front of us and the agitation showed on her face.

"Just calm down. Let the kids watch TV for a little while."

My father considered what my mom said as "back talk." He told her that she should never back talk a man and if any woman ever does than she deserved to get her ass whooped.
At that moment it was like the air had been sucked out of the room.

We all knew what was coming next.

He told my mom to lift her head up so that he can see the lips that she used to back talk him with. Slowly she closed her eyes and tilted her head up to the ceiling. With no hesitation my father punched her in the mouth and three teeth flew to the wall. The fact that Trè and I were sitting on the bed watching him hit our mom didn't seem to bother him one bit.

Scenes like this were actually normal for us, well for me anyway. Usually my mom didn't fight back; she just cried and begged him not to hit her again. Shortly after, my father ended up leaving only to return and apologize but something told him that my mom was fed up this time. He had the door of their room cracked open.

I stood at the cracked door peeking in to see what he would do next. He took out a gun out of the bureau and put it to my mom's head.

"Woman, if you ever leave me or think about leaving me, I'll kill you." He cocked the gun back and if looks could kill, my mom would have been dead.

Ma sat perfectly still with the gun pointed at her temple. She was facing the door and I could see her looking at me.

She didn't know what to do or say so she sat there with tears pouring down her blank face. I'll never forget the look in my mom's eyes. She was fed up and scared for her life. I went into my room and tried to go to sleep but I was scared for my mom's life as well as Três and mine.

Daddy finally fell into a drunken sleep and that night, my mother pulled herself together and decided that she had taken her last beating. She had us pack our bags in the middle of the night and we made our get away. My mom was crying as if somebody died while we drove away from what was now about to be our old life. All my mom kept saying to Trè and I was, "I'm sorry, I'm so sorry!"

Trè and I held hands in the back seat crying quietly. I really didn't know if I was crying because we left my father or because my mom was so hurt. My mom is a strong beautiful black woman. When I say beautiful, I mean it literally. She had us at a young age and never lost her looks. She's a beautiful caramel complexion with long jet black hair, a slender figure and a smile to light up every bad situation. Daddy is indescribable, its' a shame that the only thing I remembered about him is the constant beatings that he gave my mom. Over time my father became a monster to me and I lost all feelings for him. Every time he got paid, he would give my mom his check to go pay the bills, then he would go out get drunk and come home and ask for the check back. After developing a crack addiction in addition to the alcohol, things got worse. One time he was so drunk, he used me as an ashtray and put out his cigarette on my arm. I don't know if he was too drunk to realize what he had done or if he just didn't like me. Whatever the case may have been leaving him was the best decision my mom ever made. I was only six years old and Trè was eight. We didn't really realize how much our lives were about to change.

Most of my family lived in Boston, so my mom figured that it would be best that we moved closer to them. We ended up staying with my aunt for only a short while because she kept too much traffic flowing through her house while my mom was out looking for work.

She would literally sit with her crack-head friend's side-by-side next to Trè and me and smoke crack. They would burn a hole on the side of plastic soda bottles and smoke crack out of them. Till this day I still remember what the crack aroma smells like from staying with my aunt. At the time, I was too young to realize how much my aunt was disrespecting us, but I never respected her again after exposing us to that bullshit. Ma had too much pride to ask any other family members if we could stay with them, so we began moving from shelter to shelter. One day I got up the nerve to ask her what was going on.

"Why do we have to live in buildings with other families?" I asked.

Ma responded, "Baby, it's only temporary."

My brother Trè on the other hand was getting older and started becoming embarrassed when his friends would ask why they couldn't come to our house to play.

We were on the school bus on our way to school when two of Trè's friends decided to put our business on front street.

"I heard y'all lived in a shelter," He laughed. "Ha ha, y'all are poor!"

Trè's other friend spotted an empty soda can in the middle of the school bus aisle. He got out of his seat and gave the empty can a stern kick. As it flew to the front of the bus, he laughed and blurted out, "Oops! I just kicked your house!"

All of the kids on the school bus were cracking up adding fuel to the fire.

Trè balled his fists and turned up his face. He was about to let his anger get the best of him but instead he waited till he got home and vented out on my mom.

"Ma, we should have just stayed with Dad, at least we had our own space, I hate this shelter, I hate Boston period!"

My mom looked at him and I could see the sadness in her eyes. "Baby, even though we had a place to live when I was with your father didn't mean that we were happy."

I knew we were about to hear a lecture, but I was open to hear what my mom would say because it always seemed to make situations better.

"You two sit down," she said, directing us to sit on the hard twin bed that the shelter provided for Trè and I to share. "What doesn't kill us will make us stronger and right now you may hate where we live but I'm bursting my butt working at the Daycare during the day and Boston City hospital at night so trust me; when I say this is temporary, that's just what it is."

I went to bed that night dreaming of the day that we would have our very own apartment.

One month later it finally happened.

The apartment was a bit run down and the fact that we had to roommate with mice and roaches didn't bother us one bit because it was ours.

Trè and I had our own room and Ma looked forward to decorating the shabby apartment into making it comfortable for us. It had three bedrooms which were no bigger than a rich persons walk in closet. Even Ma's master bedroom was as small as mine and Trè's. The bathroom had the old claw foot tub and a rusty porcelain sink. There was mildew on some of the walls and the apartment's old windows didn't keep much of the cool air out.

Our first night there, my mom called Trè and I into the living room and we stood in a circle and held hands as our mom led us in prayer. She thanked God for our new apartment and for our life, health and strength. When I went into my room the very first night staying in our new apartment, I cried. I knew that my mom worked her ass off to get us this apartment and as I lay on my blanket that I temporarily used for a bed for almost a year, I was thankful. No more sharing bathrooms and kitchens with other families. Trè, Ma and I were together and starting the beginning of our new life.

Since we had our own apartment my mom decided to sign up for private childcare instead of working at the daycare center. Her plan was to do it from our apartment. She got hand-me-down toys from the last shelter that we stayed at and set up a daycare area in our living room. Eventually she quit the night job at the hospital because she thought that the private daycare would pick up and generate a ton of income.

Unfortunately the only income my mom was generating was welfare.

When Ma would send Trè and me to the store, we would try and make sure none of our friends were there when we went. If they were, we would try to stall time and look at cereal boxes a little bit longer until they left because we didn't want them to see us buying food with food stamps.

Sometimes she would send us to the store with food stamps *and* rolls of pennies; it was the most embarrassing thing I had ever experienced. We felt like a hookers going to church with their pimps. I was even embarrassed to present them to the store clerk but I knew we had to.

When we got to the age where we started to recognize named brand clothing, we realized that our clothes weren't as up to date as the other kids in the neighborhood and they had no problem pointing that out to us and Trè had no problem with knocking them out. It was obvious that Trè had a ton of anger from our situation as well as from the fact that we had an asshole for a father. I even got in tussles with a few girls around our new neighborhood.

One day two girls decided that they wanted to recite a famous song to me about my sneakers. They were snapping their fingers and singing in my face, "Boe boe's, they cost a penny and a dime, boe boe's they make your feet feel fine!"

I didn't even let them finish the song; I picked up a nice sized rock and threw it at one of the girls hitting her in the eye. She ran home crying hysterically and the other girl told me that she was going to beat me up for throwing a rock at her sister. She pushed me to the ground and I grabbed one of her legs and took her down with me. We were both on the ground rolling in the dirt for a second before I managed to end up on top of her. I took off one of my shoes and started smacking her in the face with it.

"How do these boe boe's feel across your face?" I yelled.

Trè must've seen the fight from up the street and ran down to pull me off of her. The anger behind the smacks with my shoe was fierce. I was so mad at her for teasing me that I wished I had a brick in my hand.

Trè and I begged Ma for new up to date brand name clothes and sneakers. I knew that our begging would stress her because she could barely afford to feed us, let alone buy us a pair of hundred dollar sneakers. Thank God for bootlegged clothing! Ma bought us fake Timberland and Tommy sweaters from the men selling clothes out of the trunk of their cars in Mattapan. She used to hustle those men down to the bone; sometimes she was able to get shirts for as low as five dollars.

Trè and I rocked our clothes with pride because we knew our mom was struggling because she went days without eating and got as thin as a crack head just to keep clothes on our backs and food in our bellies. Even though we were thankful for our fake wears, I could tell that Trè yearned for more. As young as he was, the gold chains on rappers and street hustlers started to appeal to him. Local hustlers started calling him "Little Man" and if they spotted us going to the store, they would pull over in their fancy cars and give us both twenty dollars a piece. Twenty dollars was a lot of money for both of us. For me it meant more candy and junk food at the store and for Trè it meant the beginning of a good idea. He saved all the money that the drug dealers gave him, birthday money and our seldom allowance and had about two hundred dollars saved and a plan to make it triple if he could.

Chapter 2 – Trè's Plan

My favorite cousin Tamika came over to chill at my house on a Friday night. We were taking turns reading each other's diary and laughing. We were like sisters, I knew all of Tamika's secrets, and she knew all of mine. She wasn't my real cousin, but we told everyone at school and in neighborhood that we were because of our strong bond.

The truth was, we met in one of the shelters that we lived in and our moms clicked just like we did. We even resembled each other; we were both slim with shoulder length silky jet black hair and were always called "the two pretty girls that were always together."

We put our diary's down and began looking for the next activity; I decided to look through Trè's closet to find something to do. As I shoved over a bunch of games on the top shelf of his closet I knocked over a shoe box full of money. I picked it up and started stuffing the bills that fell on the floor back inside of the box.

"Trè, where did you get all this money?" I asked.

"Mind your business," he said, snatching the box from me as if I was about to take it and split it with Tamika.

Tamika and I went back into my room looking at each other like we had just saw a million dollars. Trè and I were close and I couldn't wait to ask him where all that money came from and what he planned to do with it. Usually I would beg my mother to let Tamika stay the night, but on this particular night I couldn't wait for her to leave.

That night it took forever for her mother to come get her and as soon as she left, I rushed to Trè's room to interrogate him about the money. I was just about to bust in his room when I noticed that he was on the phone whispering to someone, so instead I stood by the door and quietly listened to his conversation.

I heard him say the name "John" and the only John that I could think of was the twenty something year old drug dealer that we knew from around our neighborhood.

I heard him ask, "How much can I get for it?"

Now I was pretty street savvy for my age and I knew that he meant his money and how much drugs he could get. He told John that he'd meet him at the park next to the corner store and hung up the phone. He grabbed his coat and rushed past me towards the front door.

"Where are you going Trè?" I asked, stopping him in his tracks.

"Tiara, I told you to mind your business." He adjusted his jacket and looked down the hall towards my mom's room. "Tell Ma that I'll be right back, I'm going to the park real quick."

I stood there dumbfounded as he rushed out the door.

Trè knew not to tell Ma that he was going to the park at that hour because she wouldn't have let him leave. It was either just leave, or tell me to tell Ma for him.

I went into Ma's room to relay the message from Trè and noticed she was sitting on her bed staring at a white object in her hand practically in tears.

I sank down on the bed next to her. "Ma what's wrong?"

She sniffed and wiped a tear that fell from one eye. "Baby, tell Trè to come here, I have to talk to y'all."

"Ma, Trè left, he told me to tell you that he was going to the park real quick." I knew she was about to yell so I braced myself.

"The park! It's after ten o'clock!"

She closed her eyes putting her head into her palms. "I don't know what has gotten into that boy but he is not too old to get beat."

I quickly got a flash back of how she used to give us those old school beatings. I felt bad thinking that Trè would receive one when he got home. Ma used to get a switch off of a bush outside, clean off the leaves and tear our little asses up. Sometimes it even left little red welt marks on our skin. When she didn't use a switch it was leather belts or even worse, extension cords. I tried my best to avoid whippings but Trè on the other hand stopped crying during whippings, I should've known back then he was crazy.

"Tiara, I'm pregnant."

Her words took me by surprise snapping me out of my trip down memory lane.

My mom grabbed one of my hands. "Tiara, don't let my actions be an example for you, I don't want you to be like me, I want you to be better than me. I'm not married to Orlando and neither of us have two pennies to rub together, but we are going to make this work, I promise."

I was at a lost for words. Even though we had left my father, this new baby was coming from another man and for some reason I was hurt. Orlando was a guy that worked at the agency where my mom went through for the private daycare. He was a handsome older guy, half Puerto Rican, half black with curly hair and smooth brown skin, he wasn't too tall but for the most part he was an alright guy. Or so I thought.

When Trè came back home, it was past midnight and he tried to creep in quietly but my mom was up waiting. She flicked on the light and let him have it. I snuck into the hallway and watched the whole thing.

"You think you're grown?" She nudged his head back after each sentence. "You think you're a man?"

"Ma chill, I didn't realize how late it was." Trè had one hand up trying to block my mom from hitting his forehead. I noticed his other hand was up to his jacket trying to hide a bulge confirming his little trip to meet John.

He managed to get through my mom's wrath and make it to his room. I spied on him as he hid the drugs and made his way to my mom's room after.

Trè crept in her room slowly. "Ma I'm sorry." I knew he felt bad for stressing her out.

"Trè, all the gunshots we hear around here at night, all the violence around here, why would you worry me like that?"

Trè interrupted, "There's no need to worry about me Ma, I'm a man."

My mom chuckled. "Trè, you have a long way to go to become a man, but right now I need you more than ever, we all need you." She took a deep breath. "I'm pregnant."

Trè stepped up closer to my mom. "By that nigga Orlando?" He scrunched up his face.

"Yes by Orlando Trè."

Trè calmed down and reached to hug my mom. "Don't worry about nothing, I got you."

As I made my way back to my bed I knew deep down that Trè meant exactly what he said.

Soon he started nickel and diming weed in our neighborhood. John the drug dealer took Trè under his wing, sort of like his protégé. Trè was the youngest drug dealer I knew. And as much as I knew what he was doing was wrong, I respected it. He made sure that he copped himself a big ass gold rope chain and for my twelfth birthday he promised to buy me my first pair of bamboo gold earrings.

My mom was actually further along in the pregnancy than we all had thought. She had my baby brother Sharod right before I turned twelve. He was light brown with beautiful black curly hair, he looked like a baby doll and I adored him. Orlando quickly grew attached to Sharod and moved in with us, until Trè changed things.

For some reason Orlando never liked Trè, he knew that Trè was selling drugs and kept trying to tell my mom who was in denial. Ma knew that Trè didn't get his chain or my earrings by shoveling snow for neighbors or helping them with their grocery bags, but that's what he would tell her. I think she made herself believe it since she knew that she needed the hundred dollars Trè gave her every week. Orlando's job paid him chump change and even so, he was as cheap as a kid with candy and he never helped my mom with the bills.

One day Trè and I came in from school and we overheard my mom and Orlando arguing.

"You know your son is out there up to no good and I don't want Sharod around that little nigga! He's gonna grow up to be a damn thug and you have no control over him!"

Orlando made a bad decision that day by saying that because Trè heard everything he said and he rushed into my mom's room to confront him.

"You got something to say nigga? I don't see you bringing no dough in this house so don't worry about what I'm doing!"

Orlando replied calmly, "Trè, get out of my face, this is between your mom and me."

My mom tried to pull Trè out of Orlando's face but his feet stayed planted on the ground, his face frowned and eyebrows squinted looking like he was about to hit Orlando.

Orlando grabbed his coat and left, he said that he had to drive around and get some air.

"Ma I don't like that dude," Trè said looking out the window at Orlando get into his car.

"I don't either," I chimed in, agreeing with Trè as usual.

My mom grabbed Sharod who was in his crib crying and told us that she would never let a man come between us. She told us that her kids came first and that's exactly what she meant.

When Orlando came back, my mom had his clothes packed by the door. I'll never forget the look on his face as he came through the door and saw his clothes in suitcases and bags. He looked like a child being kicked out with no where to go.

He stormed into my mom's room. "So you're kicking me out? What about Sharod can we at least work it out for him?"

My mom shouted, "Hell no!" She only cursed when she was mad so I knew she was fed up. "I'm tired of the disrespect, you come in this house, you speak to me and Tiara and you act like Trè doesn't exist. No matter what opinion you have about my son, you have to respect him, he's my child and he's apart of me. You have always had something negative to say about Trè from the beginning!"

"Fuck it! You want to act like a bitch, I'll treat you like one!"

Their voices grew louder and I ran to my mom's room and stood at the door.

Orlando kept yelling. "Fuck you and your no good ass son, and NO I never did like him because he will never amount to shit but being a hoodlum!"

My mom charged at Orlando like a football player but she was so petite he didn't even budge. Instead he grabbed her with one hand and back handed her with the other. I ran to Trè's room to tell him what had happened.

"Trè, Orlando just hit Ma!"

He instantly grew angry and rushed to the kitchen and grabbed one of the wooden kitchen table chairs. The next thing I knew he had cracked Orlando in the head with it and it turned into an all out rumble. Orlando tried to reach for Trè and I crawled over to bite Orlando's legs while my mom was punching him in the back.

"Get out Orlando, get the fuck out!" My mom screamed at the top of her lungs.

Orlando finally managed to get to the door, he grabbed his bags and headed down the stairs.

Trè stood at the top of the stairs glaring at him. "If you ever come back around here again, I'll kill you."

Orlando didn't say anything; he just shook his head in disgust and left.

About six month's later, Ma met a new dude named Primo. Primo was from the hood, he was about seven years younger than my mom but he made her happy, well for the time being. Primo was selling drugs and even doing some business with Trè on the low. If Ma had ever known about his side dealings with Trè, he would have been kicked to the curb faster than he could blink his puppy dog eye lashes. He had eye lashes like a girl, a muscular build but he was kind of chubby and always tried to walk with a gangster swagger like he was still down. And he was another cheap one. For some reason Ma always found the cheap men that didn't help her with any of the bills. He made all that money from selling drugs but instead of helping my mom, he figured that taking us out to eat here and there was enough to keep us all content.

When Primo started bringing his friends to the crib, Trè and I stopped feeling him. Everyday we would come home from school and about five niggas were in our living room smoking weed, playing video games and eating up all of our damn food. Ma worked too hard to provide for us and Trè was starting to take it personal. One day he took it upon himself to check Primo.

True enough Primo was our mother's man, but they weren't married and he wasn't our father, Trè still felt like that was his position, the man of the house. And the fact that Primo ran the streets and did business with Trè didn't make Trè respect him any more as a father figure.

Trè waved his hand and signaled for Primo to come in his room, "Can I talk to you for a minute?" Primo passed the video game controller to his partner in crime Prince and he began playing with one of their other friends.

Prince was always at our crib, whenever we saw Primo we saw Prince. They spent more time together than Primo spent with Ma. Prince was real dark skinned like burnt chocolate. He wore a lot of jewelry with sparkling diamonds. His favorite piece of jewelry was this pinky ring with a blinged out letter "P" smothered in baguettes. He would often rub his hand over his fade just to draw attention to his ring and he spoke with a southern accent. To me, he looked like an ex-crack head and I never trusted him.

Primo got up and walked in the room with Trè. My nosy ass stood outside the door to listen, I heard Trè speak first.

"Dog, what's up with you having all these niggas in the crib everyday?"
Primo chuckled, "I live here too Partna, this is my domain."

"This is your domain huh? So how much do you be putting down to stay here?" Trè asked.

I heard complete silence. I could tell Primo hesitated because Trè caught him off guard with that question.

"Don't get it twisted Trè, your mom is well taken care of." Primo said trying to sound cocky.

"I can't tell, from what I see, I'm the one holding it down around here."

Primo chuckled again, "So what are you saying lil man, since you give your mom that chump change you have the right to tell a grown man what to do?"

At this point, I poked my head in the room to watch. I saw Trè turn his head side to side looking in the back of him. "I don't see any other man in this room besides myself."

Primo put his hands up in front of him, "On that note, I'm out of here."

I quickly ran to my room as Primo turned around to go back into the living room.

Trè's pep talk must've left an impression on Primo. He didn't start helping Ma with the bills but the only company he brought over from there on out was Prince. Trè stopped doing business with Primo

and their relationship grew distant. I even overheard
Trè and one of his friends speak about robbing
Primo, but it never happened.

I was turning thirteen and was excited
because my mom told me that I could get my nose
pierced for my birthday. Trè gave me twenty dollars
so I decided that I'll spend the other ten dollars
getting Tamika's nose pierced too. Tamika was
excited to come over to show me what she got me
for my birthday. She had a bag in her hand and
anxiously handed it to me.

"Happy birthday cuz."

I grabbed the bag and looked at Tamika.
"What is it? You ain't got no money to be buying
me anything."

"Just open it!" Tamika insisted.

I opened the bag and pulled out two white
dresses and two white pairs of flip flops.
Tamika was cheesing from ear to ear, "You like
them? We are going to dress alike today."
I was as happy as a pig in shit, new outfits didn't
come my way too often.

32

"Who bought this for us, your mom?" I asked.

Tamika gave me a sly look, "Naw, I stole them."

"Tamika!" I threw her dress at her.

"What? How else was I gonna get them, I stole them from the ten dollar store downtown, ain't they fresh?"

I held my dress up in front of me, "Yeah they are cute but you don't need to be stealing Tamika."

"Tiara please, the only time we get new gear is when we get school clothes. If you don't want it you don't have to take it." She got an attitude and I could tell that I had hurt her feelings.

I snatched my dress behind my back. "You ain't taking my dress, I'm rocking this today."

Tamika smiled, "A'ight let's change and go outside to show off."

This was a treat for Tamika and I, kids in my neighborhood didn't get new clothes unless it was on a holiday. We knew we had to floss our stolen ten dollar dresses to get the other girls in the neighborhood jealous.

I spotted my friend Tammy sitting on her porch, she looked a little sad. Tammy was what you would call a fast developer. She was built like a brick house and was only thirteen. Everyone always thought that she was older than what she was because of her voluptuous shape. Tamika and I began walking towards her, I couldn't hide the fact that I wanted to show off because my smile was bigger than my face.

"Hey Tammy." I said.

Her eyes bucked when she saw our dresses. "Those dresses are dope, where did y'all get those from?"

"Don't worry about all that." Tamika said taking a seat next to Tammy on the porch.

"I was just asking." Tammy said.

"And I was just telling you." Tamika freshly replied.

Anyone that Tamika felt was getting too close to me as a friend, she would treat them like a step child because she felt that they just wanted to take her spot.

Tammy looked at me, "Well anyways, happy birthday Tiara."

"Thank you." I smiled.

She looked at my nose, "I thought you were getting your nose pierced for your birthday?"

"I am, I'm going to get it done a little later." I said.

Tamika interrupted, "Yup, we are going together to get *our* nose pierced." She said proudly. She always wanted to make my other friends feel like they were second best when it came to her. Tammy frowned up her face again and I could tell that something was bothering her.

"What's wrong with you Tammy, you okay?" I asked. Her eyes started to water and she became extremely sentimental. She began to speak and I could hear the knot in her throat.

"I-I." She struggled to get her words out.

"Damn Tammy stop stuttering and tell us what's wrong!" Tamika demanded. I bucked my eyes at Tamika, I wanted her to chill out with the rude ass comments and she shrugged her shoulders at me.

"Go ahead Tammy, tell us what's wrong." I said.

She finally let it out, "I-I got pregnant by John."

My mouth fell open and the first thought that came across my mind spilled out of my mouth.

"So you're having sex?" The answer was obvious but I just couldn't imagine someone my age laying down with a man.

She spoke through her tears, "He was my first, he told me everything that I wanted to hear, he told me that I was pretty and he made me feel good."

"Damn Tammy, what did your Mama say about this?" I asked. Tammy had one of those mothers that would come up to your school with rollers in her head cursing out the teacher whether her child was right or wrong. But she was also the type of mom that would whoop Tammy's ass with a broom, brush or whatever else she could get her hands on.

"I didn't tell her yet." Tammy said wiping her tears. "I don't know how to bring it to her. How do you think I should tell her Tiara? I don't know what to do."

Tamika watched on us as we were talking and she felt like she wasn't included in the conversation, so she decided to do what she did best, make Tammy feel like an unimportant friend.

She butted in, "Well Tammy, you shouldn't have opened your legs in the first place and you wouldn't be in this situation right now." She got up and started walking off the porch.

Tammy was speechless but not shocked at Tamika's smart comment. I rolled my eyes at Tamika as she walked off the porch.

"Anyways girl, you just have to tell her, she's going to bug out but you have no other choice."

"You ready Tiara?" Tamika said, rushing my conversation with Tammy.

I ignored Tamika and continued to listen to Tammy.

"I'm going to tell her now because I want to get it over with. I'm just going to sit here for a little while to get myself together first."

"Alright, take your time, but make sure you tell her today. Does John already know?"

She bucked her eyes wide open. "No, I didn't tell him either." I could see the fear in her eyes.

"Girl you better grow some balls." I said.

"I know, I wanted to tell my mom first though, I'm scared of what John is going to say, I'm a minor, he could get in trouble for this.

Tamika grew even more impatient. "Come on T!" She shouted from the sidewalk.

"Alright Tammy, let me go before I kill this girl, you stay strong okay?"

She looked at me with sorrow in her eyes, "Thanks T."

I walked off the porch and started walking back to my house with Tamika.

"Tamika, you know you ain't right for that."

She looked at me, "Come on T, let's be honest, she's a ho, she shouldn't have been rolling with John anyway, she got low self-esteem you could tell. She just let him hit it to fit in so fuck her."

I chuckled, "Tamika, I don't know where the hell I found you at but you are such a mess."

"What?" she said shrugging her shoulders as if she was oblivious to her rudeness.

I shook my head and chuckled and we went into the house. I yelled down the hall, "Maaa! We are going to get our nose pierced." My mom came out of her room gazing at Tamika and me.

"Y'all are not going downtown by yourselves."

"Ma, you ain't even dressed, the store will be closed by the time you get ready." I whined.

"Well you better see if Trè would go with y'all."

"Ma, you know Trè ain't gonna bring us."

Primo walked out of my mom's room rolling a blunt and Prince came strolling out after him. "I'll take them, I have to drop Prince off on Tremont Street anyway."

I got excited, "See Ma, Primo is going to bring us." I wanted my nose pierced so bad, I didn't care who was taking us.

Tamika and I went outside and sat inside of Primo's hoopty. He drove an old Ford Escort that was falling apart. His bumper was hanging off, none of the windows rolled down and the seats looked like a cat had shredded them. I always wondered where all his money went. One thing's for sure, it didn't go to my mom, nor did it go to his raggedy-ass whip. Tamika and I sat in the backseat and put on our seatbelts, Primo and Prince sat in the front bringing the weed aroma in the car with them. Their eyes were bloodshot red and they spoke about stopping by the liquor store before heading downtown. I turned up my lips in the backseat looking at the man who was a huge disappointment to me. My mom deserved so much better than

Primo, he was selfish, arrogant and disrespectful and was always drunk and high.

We stopped at the liquor store and Prince got out to get Primo two forty-ounce bottles of Old English and a few nips of Vodka. When he returned to the car, he handed Primo the bag from the liquor store. Primo reached in it and was about to twist the top off of his forty.

"I hope you ain't gonna drink that while driving with us in the car." I said giving him a funky attitude. He smirked and put the bag down. Prince watched as he put down the bag and laughed. He turned up the music and tried to drown out his words, "I don't know how you can deal with a woman with kids," he said.

Primo shifted towards Prince to whisper his response over the music, "I don't know I deal with the lil muthafuckas either." But I heard him loud and clear and I officially couldn't stand him.

When we got downtown, Tamika and I waited in line to get our nose pierced and I was steaming hot from hating Primo.

"Calm down Tiara, your mom isn't going to be with him long anyway." Tamika assured me.

"If I could help it that nigga will be getting out of our house today."

When it was my turn to get my nose pierced, I couldn't even feel it, I was so mad at the fact that Primo disrespected my mom by talking shit about her kids that I ignored the pain.

Tamika's mom happened to be downtown, she spotted us and walked into the store, she looked at Tamika's nose and snatched her up.

"Who the hell told you that you can get your nose pierced!" She yelled.

"Mom, I told you that I was going with Tiara today." Tamika lied.

Her mom yanked her arm and started pulling her out of the store, "I didn't tell your little lying ass that you could get your nose pierced."

Primo and Prince were chuckling while they stood against the wall waiting for us.

"Bye Tamika, I'll call you later." I said as her mom yanked her out of the store.

I dreaded my ride back home with Primo and Prince, we had been past Tremont Street and Prince decided that he didn't want to get dropped off anymore, he told Primo that he wanted to ride with him to make a few of his runs. My blood boiled, these niggas were really taking me on some of their drug runs and I was pissed! I thought to myself, only if my mom knew about this. After about the third stop, I started getting tired, I could smell the liquor on their breath and I knew that they were both drinking and even worse Primo was driving drunk. Before I knew it I was knocked out. When I fell fast asleep, I remember Primo leaving Prince and I alone as he entered a building to serve a play. I had to be asleep for a good ten or fifteen minutes until I felt something strange wake me up out of my sleep. I looked down and saw a hand with a sparkling "P" pinky ring going down my open jeans. I started screaming and going hysterical. Prince was trying to molest me and I wasn't having it. I reached for Primo's empty bottle of Old English and cracked it over his black ass face and it didn't even break. I managed to get out of the car and I ran as fast as I could until I reached my house. I was crying and shocked, I don't know how long I was being fondled by Prince, I wondered what else he had done to me while I was asleep. I banged on the front door and told my mom what happened and I begged her not to tell Trè. After that day, I never heard from Primo and Prince again. Primo never even showed up to get his clothes, he probably thought that Trè found out what happened and was scared for his life. But after Primo, Ma never brought another man home.

Chapter 3 – The Crew

People started to recognize and respect Trè as a money maker as well as someone who was protected. John and his crew made sure that no one fucked with Trè. John even gave him his first gun which he quickly came home and showed to me. "Tiara, this is a two-two, what you know about this?" he asked bragging.

"You better not let Ma see that." I instructed.

"I won't, and you better not tell her either." Trè handed the gun to me to examine.

Unfortunately that wasn't the last gun that I saw. Trè started getting them more often. Not to use, he didn't have any enemies at the time, I think he was just fascinated with them. He was making so much money that he was spending it on any and everything. My mom started worrying because he started coming in later and later every night. She didn't care about the hundred dollars a week anymore; it was about Trè's future.

One night he came in after midnight and my mom was more than fed up. She confronted him hoping to get through to him.

"Trè, I know that fast money is more appealing than working for it, but you have so much life to live Baby, you can end up dead or in jail. What kind of example are you setting for Tiara and Sharod?"

"I'm a man Ma, I have to do this."

"Stop telling me that you're a man, you're still a kid."

Trè's anger grew and he started to raise his voice. "I am a man! I make more than some kid's fathers and I'm not even fourteen yet. I buy my own clothes and I even buy clothes for Sharod and Tiara and I help you with the bills!"

"Okay Trè, you're a man? Then leave," she snapped. "You wouldn't survive one day without me. Money doesn't make you a man, remember that."

"I don't have time for this Ma, I'm out." Trè headed for the door.

"Don't leave Trè." I cried. I hated when they argued.

Trè stormed out the door as I tried to console my mother.

During my mom and Trè's argument I had heard ambulance and police sirens but I ignored it because it was nothing unusual to hear it in Dorchester, but the sirens sounded a bit too close.

About an hour later Trè came in the house in tears. My mom had already cried herself to sleep but I was up waiting for Trè.

"What's wrong Trè, what happened?" Trè wasn't the type to cry so I knew it had to be something serious.

"Somebody killed John," he said as tears began streaming down his face.

"What? When? What happened?" I had just seen him earlier in the day.

"Somebody shot him five times right up the street." Trè sniffed. "This is fucked up Tiara that was my dog, he was like an older brother to me."

"I'm sorry Trè." I hugged him mainly because I didn't know what else to do. This was the first time that someone I knew got killed, but deep down I knew he wouldn't be the last. I thought about Tammy and the baby that she was carrying and I felt bad. Her poor baby would be deemed a bastard in society and it's not even the baby's fault.

I later found out that Tammy's mom moved her whole family down south. They wanted no parts of whatever problems that John had on the streets and I never saw Tammy again.

When my mom found out about John, she found another apartment quick. She was finally accepted by Section-8 so she was able to afford the rent at our new place. The apartment was still in Dorchester but it was closer to Mattapan. The neighborhood was even worse than where we lived previously but my mom didn't care, she just wanted to get Trè away from John's crew because she knew they were thinking of retaliating.

Unfortunately we had to change schools, but thankfully I was enrolled in the same school as Tamika. I became popular quick, especially due to the fact that I was Trè's sister. All the girls liked Trè because he made money and he was fine as hell. Well that's what they all said, to me, he was just my brother. He was just starting to grow his braids and the clothes he wore always complimented his natural muscular build. Even Tamika had a crush on Trè but he always said that she was too young for him, plus it would have messed up our fake cousin image. Tamika loved to visit us at our new place. It was a brick apartment building that housed about nineteen apartments. It wasn't the projects but it may as well been. If we were to walk to any of the corner stores or liquor stores, we would have to pass the projects.

Tamika and I befriended other girls from the projects as well as in my apartment building. We even formed a crew and called ourselves "Dime

Piece Gangstresses" or "DPG."

Every female crew has a neutral chick, hoodrat, chickenhead, thorough chick and a bitch in the crew. Tamika and I were neutral, I was a mix of all of the above except I had too much respect for myself to be a ho, Tamika was a mix of everything, she had shady, sneaky ways to her but just enough to be neutral.

Then we had Ke-Ke, she put the *hood* in hoodrat. The words: nigga or dog was used after all of her sentences. She had a body shaped like a Coca-Cola bottle, a huge butt and an attitude to match the screw face she kept. Renée was the chickenhead, she had a figure similar to Ke-Ke's but she had a bigger chest. She loved to flaunt it every chance she got. She was always in guy's faces and fucked too many niggas to name in the projects. I made her slow that shit down when she became apart of the crew though. Shavon was the thorough chick; she was the biggest one out of all of us. When we had drama with other chicks and they found out that we rolled with Shavon they would try

50

to squash that beef quick. She fucked up mad bitches and she was my roll dog.

Last but not least there's Karen, the bitch. She had no butt, no chest but her face was beautiful in comparison to Halle Berry or Beyoncè. But the screw face she wore on it even outdid Ke-Ke's. She kept an attitude and she didn't like anyone except us it seemed. She was rude as shit to other people, I didn't even like her when I first met her but we eventually became close.

I formed our crew because I envied Trè's new crew and how he was a leader like John was. He took everything John taught him and applied it to his crew and I took everything that I learned from Trè and applied it to mine, however Trè and his boys were grimy. The grimier his crew got, the grimier mine got.

In Boston, most crews are set up by street names also known as blocks. If you walked down the wrong block and niggas didn't know you, you could get robbed just like that.

Trè's crew was known for being "stick up kids". They were robbing everyone and at the same time gaining enemies.

Ke-Ke and I decided to take a walk to Trè's block one day to see if we could get some money from him. On the way, we were talking about the guys we were trying to lock down.

"What's up with your boy Jason, tell that nigga to hook me up with his fine ass brother Kevin." Ke-Ke laughed.

"Girl please, Jason is just my friend and his brother ain't even cute, you better stick to talking to Jizz."

"Aw, T you hating dog."

We both laughed.

Just as we bent the corner we saw Trè's friend Taqwon with a gun up to some girl's head robbing her for her bamboo earrings. The girl was crying and screaming and I could tell from the look on her face she was scared for her life.

Taqwon hit her in the head with his gun. "Shut up Bitch!"

Ke-Ke and I stood there frozen watching the whole thing. Her eyes were wide open, "Oh hell no, you peep that shit T?"

Ke-Ke slowly walked backwards.

"Yeah I saw that shit, is that Trè across the street?"

Ke-Ke looked across the street. "That damn sure is Trè." She grabbed the back of my shirt. "Tiara, let's go nigga, this is some crazy shit."

Trè was across the street robbing what looked like the girl's boyfriend. He had the dude face down on the side walk with his gun pointed at his head as he checked his pockets. Ke-Ke and I turned around and ran off the block back to my building.

I knew Trè was robbing people but that was the first time I peeped it with my own eyes. He used to bring me home earrings and other jewelry that he got from robbing people. I would gladly take them downtown to the jewelry exchanges and trade them in for the newest earrings that were out and of course I use to hook the crew up sometimes too.

Trè stopped going hard at the drug game because he had even robbed some of his customers. He was fighting all the time, robbing people, pistol whipping people and had a lot of people fearing him.

I guess Orlando was right, Trè ended up being a thug. And my young naïve ass looked to him as a role model.

Chapter 4 – Drama

On Sunday nights there was a skating rink called The Vous, (pronounced The Voo). It was a hang out to skate and dance to hip hop and R&B. It was also the spot where a lot of people had their first fist fight, including myself. I'll never forget the day Tamika and I went to The Vous without the crew and this girl Takia who Shavon had beat up before thought she caught us sleeping because her crew was deeper than we were.

Takia didn't like me because her boyfriend Chris had a crush on me. Before he became her boyfriend, he and I shared my first kiss in the hallway at school. I guess the jealousy carried over into their relationship and she told everyone that she didn't like me. Shavon seen her one day and beat her ass for telling people she didn't like me and we had drama with Takia ever since.

Chris was later killed during a shoot out with some dudes from another block. But the beef with Takia was still on. Tamika and I kept razors in our sneakers all the time just in case anything ever popped off and we were just itching to use them. After The Vous let out, Takia approached us with three other girls, two of them were punks and one of them tried to be thorough along with Takia. I started whooping Takia's ass on the spot and Tamika stomped the shit out of her other girl, one of the other punks who watched as we beat the shit out of their friends tried to be bold and run up on me after she saw that Takia was getting her ass beat too bad. I whipped out my razor and sliced a line across her face.

We ran home and Tamika was laughing hysterically. "You shoulda sliced DPG in that bitch's face so that she would always remember not to fuck with our crew."

"That bitch know the deal, she'll think of me every time she look in the mirror," I said.

I later found out that the girl whose face I sliced moved to Atlanta. Her mom didn't want to live in Boston any longer but it made Takia hate us even more.

We let a few Sunday's pass before we went back to The Vous. Renée called me amped about wearing a new outfit to The Vous that some nigga bought her.

"Tell Trè to give you the money to go to The Vous tonight."

"I'm good," I said. "I got my eight dollars to get in. Tamika should be straight too but I know the rest of the girls ain't got no money."

I suddenly got an idea. "Renée, call the girls and tell everybody to meet me here in fifteen minutes."

Karen lived upstairs in the same building that I did, Ke-Ke, Renée and Shavon lived in the projects down the street. Everyone arrived in fifteen minutes except for Renée, she was late as usual. We waited for her in the hallway of my building.

She came in walking up the hall.

"Here come Renée's late ass," Karen said rolling her eyes letting her bitchy attitude show in her words.

"Shut up Karen, you can't rush perfection," Renée turned around to model the outfit she got from some random nigga.

"Your outfit's a'ight, it ain't nothing special, tell that nigga to step up his game and buy you some Gucci shit," Karen said.

"Bitch, you're hating as usual, fall the fuck back."

"Shut up y'all," I interrupted eager to tell them about my plan. "Now I know y'all don't have the money to get in The Vous, so peep what I think we should do, let's rob Takia." I watched for everyone's reactions.

"I'm down!" Shavon said with no questions asked.

Ke-Ke looked a little taken aback but we were a crew and if one was down then we all were.

"Well if we are gonna do this then y'all are gonna have to wait for me to change clothes," Renée's bourgeois ass said.

Karen rolled her eyes. "Here we fuckin' go."

I sucked my teeth. "Calm down, this should be easy. Takia usually picks her little sister up from that dance school on Blue Hill Ave at 4 o'clock, either she rolls with her cousin Monique or she goes by herself. We just have to lay in the cut while she's walking and she won't even see it coming," I said proudly.

"That bitch always got dough on her too, let's jack the fuck outta that ho," Karen said extending her arm out to give Shavon dap.

"A'ight y'all, it's 3:45 now, we need to start walking towards Blue Hill Ave, she's probably already walking." I looked around at everyone, they all had their game faces on. "Let's do this."

We tied our scarves on our heads and headed towards Blue Hill Ave. We found the perfect cut to hide in. It was a skinny alley way between two houses. It was the perfect spot for me to peek out to see when Takia was walking by.

When I saw Takia, I noticed that she was talking to someone, it was Monique. I turned around to let the girls know that she wasn't by herself. As soon as Takia and Monique passed the cut where we were hiding, we jumped out on them.

Shavon grabbed Takia and punched her in the face. "What now bitch?"

Takia stumbled to the ground while Karen and I got up on Monique. I punched her dead in her nose and Karen yanked her by her hair to the ground.

"Run ya shit!" Ke-Ke said forcing them to empty their pockets.

Takia was crying hysterically trying to recover from Shavon's blow to her face.

"Shut up you stupid bitch," Renée said punching her in the face again.

"Fuck y'all bitches!" Monique said trying to uphold her pride.

Ke-Ke kicked her in the face causing her head to slam against the cement. I knelt over her emptying her pockets while Shavon and Renée emptied Takia's pockets. They didn't even fight back, they were outnumbered and shit outta luck. We took all their money and their jewelry. One of the ladies that lived on the street came out of her house screaming and being dramatic, "What are y'all doing to those girls!"

That was our sign, we robbed them and it was time to bounce. We didn't want that lady calling the police. We ran down the street laughing at what we had just done yelling, "DPG, ask about us bitches!"

When we finally got back to my apartment building, we counted all the money and split the jewelry.

"That shit felt so good!" Shavon said.

"We gotta do that again, that shit was too easy nigga," Ke-Ke agreed.

Renée brushed off her shoulders. "And I didn't even get dirty."

We all laughed because she was still worried about her damn outfit.

I caught my breath. "A'ight y'all, let's go get Tamika and head to The Vous."

We fixed ourselves up, took our scarves off and headed to Tamika's.

The Vous was only a ten minute walk from Tamika's house. The girls were still amped about what we had done earlier and they couldn't wait to tell her on our way there. As we were walking, Tamika let the girls walk ahead so that she could talk to me. She had a sour attitude, and it showed in her face and tone. "Damn T, why didn't you come get me? You know I would've been down to rob these bitches."

"Yeah I knew you would've been down but I also knew you had the money to get in The Vous, so what the fuck would've been the point for you to come?" I was heated that she came out her mouth sideways.

"But T, I'm your right hand, I was around before any of them, I shoulda been the first person you called."

I became agitated. "Tamika on some real shit, it ain't that serious! Stop questioning me about this shit because you're making me mad, we did what we had to do and that's that, leave it be."

"You're right T, it's all good, I'm gonna leave it alone," Tamika said, but the jealousy still showed on her face.

Tamika's shadiness often showed even as we were older, it was like she always wanted me to herself, I loved her to death but that shit made me mad sometimes.

The drama didn't end that night. Word got back to Takia's girls about what we had done to her and Monique. Takia's girls were like ten deep at The Vous, they didn't even skate, and they stayed on the benches all night wearing shady looks on their faces. The crew and I didn't care, if it had to go down, then so be it. My girls never backed down from a fight and we were skating like we were untouchable.

Ke-Ke and Karen went to the snack bar, Renée and Tamika were still on the rink skating and Shavon and I went to the bathroom. Something told me to go to the snack bar because I knew Takia's girls were waiting for us to separate so I tried to rush Shavon out the bathroom.

"Girl, hurry up, I have a feeling that these bitches are gonna try to be on some sneaky shit."

Shavon flushed the toilet and came out of the stall fixing her pants. "Tiara if those bitches try something then it's on, we'll rob all them hoes."

"Yeah I feel you but let's just go and check on the girls in the snack bar real quick because I don't trust them bitches."

Shavon and I entered the snack bar; Ke-Ke and Karen were still in line. I skated over to them to check on them. "Y'all straight?" I gave them the look to let them know that it will go down if there was a problem.

"Yeah dog we're good" Ke-Ke said.

"A'ight I'll be over here, Karen order me a hot dog." I skated over to the chairs on the side of the snack bar where Shavon was already sitting. She was taking off her skates because her feet were hurting. About six of Takia's friends came into the snack bar. They didn't know that Shavon and I were sitting on the side so they thought that they had their chance at revenge. Karen got her food and headed towards me and Shavon when one of Takia's friends put her foot under Karen's skate and tripped her. "That's for Takia bitch!" Karen's juice, food and candy along with my hotdog fell on the floor. I tapped Shavon who was bending over pulling up her socks and told her to come on. She sat up and saw Karen on the floor and blurted, "Oh, hell no!"

We made our way over to Takia's girls, they were shocked to see that we were in the snack bar, I didn't even care about the fact that I had on skates, it was on. I punched any random chick in her face, I didn't care who it was. Ke-Ke and Karen were tussling with two girls and Shavon was trying to knock them all out like they were the ones that robbed one of us.

Next thing I knew, I had a girl on the ground pounding on her face, another girl came out of nowhere pulling my hair from behind. That's when the unthinkable happened. I don't know how Shavon made her way back to her skates but when I turned around to fight the girl that was pulling my hair, Shavon came out of nowhere and cracked her in the head with her skate. I heard a loud scream and all I saw was the girl running out of the snack bar holding her head with blood seeping through her fingers. Most of her girls followed except for the ones that Ke-Ke and Karen had on the ground stomping with their skates.

The skate was still in Shavon's hand as she held an ice grill ready to hit someone else.

"Girl put that skate down we gotta be out!" I tried to rush Shavon before someone called the police.

We all skated out of the snack bar to one of the benches and changed out of our skates. Shavon was on foot so she ran to the skating rink to get

Renée and Tamika's attention. "Come on bitches," she yelled waving her arms to get their attention.

They skated up and asked what happened.

"Yo, just take off your skates, we gotta be out," I said rushing them.

That was our last night at The Vous and Sunday nights would never be the same. As we headed home that night, we told Tamika and Renée what happened in the snack bar and they were pissed that they missed it. "Damn why do I always miss the drama?" Tamika said mad that she wasn't there to fight again.

"We held that shit down, they were deep and still couldn't see us," I said.

"Yeah and that bitch that I cracked in the head with my skate ain't gonna be seeing shit either, I left that bitch bloody," Shavon boasted.

"Shavon, you are a crazy bitch," I said looking at her.

"Nah T, when I saw that bitch pulling your hair, I got heated, you're my dog, I wanted to hurt that bitch bad."

I gave Shavon dap. "You are truly my girl for life, all of y'all are." I looked at the crew proud that I had a bunch of chicks down for each other.

I couldn't blame Shavon for her craziness. Like me, she also came from a broken home. Both of her parents were crack heads so she was raised by her grandmother. Normally when grandmothers take in their grandkids, they showed them the love that they missed out on from the absence of their parents, but Shavon's grandmother was different. She didn't give one fuck about Shavon or her sister. She never told Shavon she loved her, she never showed her any affection.

The lack of love made Shavon who she was; she was grimey, but also very protective of our crew because we were her only family. Shavon always told me that she looked up to me for my leadership and that she admired the fact that I had ambition and I was glad to take her under my wing.

The girls and I separated that night and I was finally home. Just when I thought that the drama was over for the night, Trè met me in my room. One of his boys fucked with one of Takia's girls and told him about us robbing them earlier.

"What up big bro?" I started taking off my shoes and was about to lie on my bed and relax.

"What's up with them scratches on your neck?" he said pointing to the fresh red scratches that I got from the girl pulling my hair at The Vous.

"Oh that ain't nothing, I got in a fight with some chick."

He shook his head. "That shit ain't cute Tiara."

I sat up on my bed and scrunched up my face. "Trè, I know you ain't talking!"

"What's this I'm hearing about you robbing someone? Leave that shit to niggas, girls ain't built for that. I haven't robbed anyone that I didn't have to, I do it to provide for you and the fam."

"So you're glorifying why you're doing it, what if I did it for the same reason?"

Trè was getting pissed at my smart remarks. "It ain't the same reason, if my little sis needs something then she needs to ask me and I'll give it to her," he said. "Let me be the one to get my hands dirty, not you T, you're better than these streets, shit we both are but at the end of the day, I'm a man and I couldn't call myself a man if I didn't provide for y'all."

Trè was right, I had no business out there robbing other people that were just as poor as I was. But fuck it, if I had to do it again, then I would, so Trè's words went in one ear and out the other.

Chapter 5 – Beef

I knew that robbing Takia would continue the beef that we already had amongst our girls, but I didn't care at the time. I heard that they even came to my High school like ten deep looking for me and Tamika, but we never crossed paths. Having beef on any level in the hood meant that you always had to stay on point and never get caught sleeping. Luckily as time went, the rumors died down. Some of the rumors we used to hear were crazy. Some people said that I was the one that cracked the girl in the head with my skate or that we stabbed Takia and Monique while robbing them. The rumors made girls at my school fear my crew even more, they were terrified of us. We had groupies that used to try to be down with us but we kept all outsiders at a distance. I knew my girls for too long and I trusted them.

By the time I was sixteen years old you would've thought I was twenty. Growing up rough had a way of making you age quicker. It was almost like being robbed of your youth. I didn't have positive role models and all I was trying to do was survive. My mom was still on welfare struggling with no kids enrolled in her private daycare and I didn't want to ask Trè for anymore money and I definitely didn't want to rob anyone else. I started doing things that my gut feeling told me not to do but my exterior told me that I had to. Old shoes and clothes weren't attractive on a pretty girl.

My homeboy Jason had some scams that he told me would be beneficial. He was eighteen and had a job working for a credit card company. Every week he would give me new credit card numbers and I would order sneakers and clothes from catalogs and have them sent to bogus addresses. I knew the date that the merchandise would arrive and I would meet the truck at the address before they had a chance to ring the doorbells.

I felt bad for running up people's credit card bills but Jason would always tell me, "You're only robbing from the rich."

With me being envious of rich people it made it easier not to feel bad.

Jason didn't like giving me the card numbers over the phone so I'd always go to his house on Fridays to get them. Our normal routine was for me to come over and chill while Jason smoked some weed, talk about the latest gossip, give me the card numbers and I would be out. It felt good chilling with a dude. Sometimes, it was like an outlet away from the girls every so often.

One Friday night, he switched up the whole routine. He handed me the paper with the new card number on it and I decided to leave earlier than usual that night.

"A'ight Jason I'm tired, I'm about to bounce, I'll call you when I get to the crib."

Jason stood in front of me close enough to kiss me.

"Move Jason stop playing, I gotta go." I shoved him out of my way but he didn't budge.

He frowned. "Why you always gotta go? Why can't you stay here with me, there ain't no school tomorrow?"

"Jason what do I look like staying here? For real move!" I shoved him again but he still didn't move. He took his hands and started caressing my breasts. I took a step back and I hauled off and slapped the shit out of him.

"You bitch!" he shouted. He shoved me on his bed and tried to pin my arms down but I was fighting him with everything I had. One major kick to his balls with all my might had him curled up in a ball like a baby. I made my way out the door and I made sure that I took the credit card numbers with me.

That was the end of that connect and the end of me talking to Jason. I hated when niggas acted like they couldn't just be your friend, they always wanted something in return and I wasn't the chick to give it to them. Jason was damn lucky I didn't tell Trè because that would have been his ASS! I knew that Trè would have done something to him to land him behind bars so I didn't tell him or anyone, not even my girls.

Jason ended up getting his in the end. Apparently I wasn't the only female that he was giving credit card numbers to and when one found out about the other, she decided to call his job and tell them all about their generous employee. Karma is a bitch!

Renée and Karen had another job proposition for me. They were using what they had to get what they wanted, not stripping but setting niggas up. I rode with them one day on one of their missions. Our boy Burns from around the way told them to hook up with these two niggas from Brockton. He told them that the niggas had hella dough and all they had to do was make the niggas fall in love with them so they were comfortable enough with showing them where they kept their dough, report it back to Burns and they would split it 50/50. On the way to Brockton Karen and Renée filled me in on their strategy.

Karen's bitchiness came from her mom. Her mom was the Queen bitch. As a matter of fact, ever since I known Karen, I never heard her mom refer to her as Karen, she always called her "that little bitch." My attitude would be fucked up too if my mom never respected me. Her mom never respected her as a kid, so as she was coming into her own, it was hard for her to respect herself. So fucking niggas to set them up didn't bother her, she just looked at it as a come up.

Renée was from the projects so her whole mind set was to get money. She wanted to live better and floss like she had money. I couldn't blame her, she grew up rough, shit I thought I never had anything but she had to share one bedroom with four other siblings. They shared the same clothes and shoes for years. Her apartment smelled worse than the project hallway. It always smelled like piss and shit in her spot so whenever we were there we made sure it wasn't for long.

Fucking niggas to set them up definitely wasn't anything new to Renée, she was doing that anyway. Niggas always called her a chickenhead because she was always up in some niggas face trying to get something from him.

They had already been talking to the niggas from Brockton for like 2 months now. The dudes lived together and they were both stupid enough to let Renée and Karen know where they kept their stash at in the crib. Karen told me that they sold drugs and kept them hidden in the dropped ceiling in their apartment and the money in two separate safes behind a hidden door under the kitchen cabinet. They had these niggas open! Before we left, they had called them on the phone. Renée put them on speaker so we could hear just how open they were.

"Hey papa it's Renée."

"What up baby, what time are you coming? I miss you."

"I'll be out there shortly."

"Make sure you bring over that red lingerie outfit I got you from Victoria Secret."

Renée rolled her eyes and went with the flow. "You know I'm going to wear that just for you papa."

"You wet thinking about me?"

"I'm always wet thinking about you, I can't wait to ride you daddy but afterwards you have to take me out for some seafood."

We all were trying hard to hold in our laughter.

"A'ight boo, whatever you want, you got that a'ight? See you when you get here," he said.

"Wait, Papa don't hang up, put Rico on the phone, Karen wants to talk to him."

"A'ight hold on."

We heard fumbling before Rico came across the speaker and Renée handed the phone to Karen.

"Hello?"

"Hey Rico Baby, you ready for me?"

"Yes baby, come out here, I got shit set up in the room for us. I got some porno's and some more shit." Rico's Puerto Rican accent was thick and heavy.

Karen smiled. "A'ight just make sure you set shit up right and I hope you changed the damn sheets from before," Karen snapped.

"Mama, don't worry, I got everything right for you 'kay?"

"A'ight, we still going out to get some seafood with Renée and your brother afterwards right?"

"Baby, we can do whatever you want after you break me off."

"A'ight we on our way."

Karen hung up the phone and we all fell out laughing.

"See how easy that shit was T? These niggas are so stupid they would do anything for some good pussy."

We went outside and got into the car with Burns to take us out to Brockton which was like a half hour ride. This would be the end of the faking, while Karen and Renée fucked and went out to dinner with these niggas, Burns and his boy were gonna go in the crib, take their shit and we were gonna bounce. When Karen and Renée returned from dinner, they were supposed to act surprised like they didn't know what the fuck happened.

It was the perfect scheme.

When we pulled up to their crib in Brockton, we parked on the corner.

"A'ight, do what y'all have to do and get these niggas out the house quick, we ain't trying to be out here all night. And make sure y'all stay at the restaurant as long as possible. One of y'all has to be the last one to leave to make sure y'all leave the door unlocked."

"A'ight Burns, we know the routine, it's gonna be easy, let's get this money," Karen said rushing Burns.

"A'ight, see y'all back in the Bean."

Karen and Renée looked at me. "A'ight T, be careful okay?"

That's when I suddenly realized what I was doing. While Karen and Renée was out to dinner with these dudes, I would either be in the car waiting for Burns and his boy to wipe these niggas clean or I could be in there getting mine too. I was suddenly in an uncompromising position and wasn't sure I liked the way it felt.

We waited in the car for about forty-five minutes until Karen and Renée finally came out the house with the dudes. As they walked to the car they looked at us, Karen winked giving us the signal that the door was unlocked. As soon as they pulled off, Burns and his boy got out the car, put on their hoods and ran up to the house. I was in the car looking out to see if anyone was coming.

"T, what are you doing out here? What are you going to do?" I asked myself out loud. I was nervously patting my foot on the car floor. I looked at an extra oversized hoodie that big ass Burns had in the car and said fuck it. I threw it on, pulled the hood over my head and went into the crib and tried to get me something too.

Burns and his boy were busy trying to carry the safe from under the cabinet. They had already cleared all the drugs from the dropped ceiling and had them in duffle bags. I didn't want drugs, I wanted some dough.

I went into one of the rooms, I saw a few rings with diamonds on the dresser so I swiped them and put them in my pockets. I opened the top drawer and hit the jackpot. There was a stack of money but after I counted it, it only ended up being $300.00 but I still got something out of the situation.

I went to the car before Burns and his boy got there and I couldn't wait for them to hurry the fuck up. They came out of the house each carrying the duffle bags over their shoulders and a safe in their hands. They put the shit in the back seat next to me and we sped off. Burns let his boy drive and the dumb ass nigga skidded away like someone was following us and I couldn't help but to speak up.

"What are you doing, you're making us hot?" I yelled from the backseat.

"I know what I'm doing, we have to be out!"

I sat back looking at the back of his head, I wanted to punch it, that was the dumbest move ever, the neighbors could have peeped the license plate or the jakes could have been rolling by, plus the neighborhood was already hot.

This nigga continued to speed and just as I had predicted the fucking police spotted us. I thought that we were going to lead them on a high speed chase but this nigga turned a sharp corner, stopped the car and got out and started running.

Burns was just as heated as I was but had no choice but to run. I couldn't believe I was running from the police like I was a damn thug. I was climbing fences, running through people's backyards and hiding behind shit. I was so fucking pissed that I even lost the rings that I swiped out of one of the rooms. When I was finally cleared from the police I made it to the train station. I was on the train steaming out of my mind. I knew my girls would be pissed that they put in all that work for Burn's dumb as friend to fuck everything up.

Later on that night, I watched the news, they were talking about two dudes in Brockton that were caught exiting a car with about ten keys of coke and two safes full of guns and money. Burns and his boy got caught and they were about to be serving half their lives in jail. Burns was a cool nigga, he had a lot of operations going on in the hood, so with him down meant a lot of niggas wouldn't be eating.

Later that night Karen and Renée came over.

"T, what the fuck happened?" Renée asked.

"Burns stupid ass boy was speeding like someone was chasing us, the nigga made us so hot that the police finally got a hold of our asses. We could've got away but his dumb ass decided to pull over and start running. That nigga was stupid as shit, I don't know where the fuck Burns found that non-descript nigga."

"Damn!" Karen screamed. "All that shit for nothing, fucking with them lame ass niggas for nothing?"

She sat on my bed and shook her head. "T, did you at least get something out of this?"

"Girl I got about three hundred bills, I'll give y'all both a hundred of it because y'all are my girls, we can take this loss together."

"That's real T," Renée said.

"Do you know that Rico and his brother was fuckin' crying, those niggas got cleaned out, I felt sorry for them but at the same time I was excited to meet Burns to get my cut," Karen said.

"Damn, my nigga Burns is gonna be gone for a minute, that's fucked up." Renée shook her head.

I gave them both a hundred dollars and that was the very last time that Karen and Renée set anybody up.

The incident with Jason and the crazy shit that happened with Renée and Karen forced me to try to get a legal gig for a change. Most places wanted you to be sixteen to be able to work there so I was already all set. I went to the mall and filled out applications everywhere. When I got home my mom had a note for me on my bed. It said that the Shoe Express store in the mall called for me. I was so excited that I actually got a call back on the same day.

All of my references and work history were fraudulent and I hoped that they didn't want to verify anything. If they called any of them back, they would have had the honor of speaking to Tamika, Ke-Ke, Shavon, Renée or Karen. I told the girls in advance that I would use them as a reference and prepped them on what to say in case any of the jobs called them for references. I called Shoe Express back, they told me to come in the next day for an interview. I was so happy as I laid my clothes out and prepared for the next day. I told Trè about my interview, he was very proud of me. For some reason, his approval always made me feel special.

The next day I nailed the interview by giving them the professional Tiara. All the Ebonics and hood shit went out the door. I needed the little $6.50 an hour they were offering and I was happy as hell when they hired me on the spot and asked me to start the following week.

I knew one of the other cashiers that worked there so it made work more fun. She and I spent the majority of the time gossiping when it wasn't busy.

I was popular at school so the word got out quick about where I worked. It bothered me though because I didn't like too many people knowing my business. All the girls from school used to ask for discounts on shoes and of course the crew got hooked up.

I was a bit rude to some chicks, random chicks in school would come up to me asking for my discount, they figured that this was a good way for them to try to be my friend. I would look them dead in their face and not say anything. Then they would feel stupid and turn around and walk away. Tamika peeped me in action when this chick from school that I never liked asked for a hook up. I ice grilled the chick while Tamika walked up to me and the girl walked away.

"Damn T, you're mad rude, you gave that bitch the fuck off look."

"I'm not rude, she know I don't like her, I don't even speak to her and she's asking for a hook up, come on now."

"I feel you, that discount is for DPG members only, Holla! Especially me of all people, I get the hook up first."

Typical Tamika again, always thinking that I should show her some favoritism.

"The crew got that, my girls get hooked up first, matter fact y'all should come meet me on my lunch break today so we could chill in the mall."

"Nah, Ke-Ke's cousin is having that party tonight remember? Them dudes from her cousins block are gonna be there so you know I gotta look fly."

"Damn, I forgot all about that shit, I hate working on Fridays." I said pissed that I wouldn't be able to go.

"Sorry T." Tamika stopped and did a booty dance in the hallway next to our class.

"Fuck you bitch. I need this money anyway so y'all have fun for me."

I was miserable working that Friday night. My friend, the other cashier didn't arrive until six so I was bored out of my mind with no one to talk to and the store was slow as hell.

When my friend finally came, it was like a breath of fresh air.

"Girl, it hasn't been busy in here at all, I'm glad you're here because my ass was about to fall asleep." We both started laughing.

As I turned around to help who I thought was a customer, I realized it was Takia. I thought to myself, "Oh hell no! This day couldn't have gotten any worse."

She walked up close to the register. "So this is where you work at huh bitch?"

I looked around for my manager who was thankfully in the stock room and I looked her dead in her eyes. "Bitch you must got me twisted, don't let this uniform fool you because we can get it crackin' in this store."

Takia took a step back, she smiled. "I got you Tiara, I'll see you when you get off work."

I gave her the look that could boil cold water. "Then it's on bitch!"

I don't know what the fuck I was thinking. All my girls were at Ke-Ke's cousin's party and I didn't have the phone number to reach them because her cousin and I weren't close like that. I still didn't give a fuck, beef was beef but damn why today? Takia was with two other girls and I was by myself. I put my tough act aside and started thinking rational.

Since the cashier chick wanted to be down with the crew so bad, she better have my back. She finished ringing in her customer and she turned and asked, "Who was that?"

I sucked my teeth. "That ain't nothing but this stupid bitch that me and my girls got beef with. She tried to be on some tough shit talking about she'll see me after work. Whatever's whatever, you got my back if it goes down right?"

She looked at me and gave me a shady "yes" like she was scared. I thought to myself, this bitch better not be no punk.

Ten o'clock rolled around, it was closing time. My hair was already in a ponytail so I swooped the longer piece into a bun and put on my scarf. I kept Vaseline in my purse so I put it on my face and made sure my shoe laces were tight. I clocked out and noticed my friend was stalling.

"Girl hurry up!" I insisted. I knew her ass was stalling on purpose.

We left the store and headed for the escalator. On the way down, I looked around the mall for Takia and her girls but they were no where to be found. I was actually relieved at the thought of them chickening out but that thought was quickly interrupted with a blow to the back of my head as I exited the mall to go outside. I couldn't believe these sneaky bitches waited for me on the outside of the mall.

I turned around to tussle with Takia, I wasn't a cat fight type of chick, I throw blows only, Takia on the other hand liked to scratch but I wasn't letting her hands land on me. Just when her two other friends were jumping in to help Takia, my scary ass friend took off running. I couldn't believe that bitch actually left me to get jumped by three girls.

For the most part, I was handling them, all the wrestling with Trè was paying off. They did manage to get some good blows to my face though, it was hard trying to fight and block three chicks. They almost had me backed into a corner when mall security ran outside to break up the fight.

Takia and her girls took off running when they saw security. I caught my breath, picked up my purse and walked off. Mall security was asking me questions but I ignored them and kept it moving. When I got to the bus stop, I noticed that my cashier friend was still waiting for the bus. I walked up on her and cussed her out.

"Bitch, you left me by myself to fight three girls, it would've only been two against three, if I knew you were a punk bitch I wouldn't have ever wasted my time talking to your bitch ass."

She looked at me with her eyes wide open scared out of her mind. "I'm sorry T, I got scared, I thought I seen 5-0." I couldn't believe this bitch was lying in my face. She knew she didn't see no damn police and I felt like lying was the biggest form of disrespect plus this hoe left me to get jumped. I wasn't used to being around punks, all of my girls never asked any questions and we jumped in the fight regardless of anything.

I felt sorry for my cashier friend after that because I laid the ass whopping of a lifetime on her. All she kept doing was blocking her face, I threw combinations to her face, blow after blow leaving her bloody.

When I finally made it home, my mom was up playing some old school Marvin Gaye. She had a champagne glass full of cheap wine singing the words and dancing in front of Sharod. He was on the couch giggling at her. I watched her grooving while Sharod was cracking up laughing. He was so innocent and he didn't have a care in the world. It made me wonder what kind of sister I really was. I ran the streets with the girls all day fighting for things as little as another chick looking at us wrong.

What kind of example was I being for Sharod? I still needed to play a positive role in his life. Looking up to Trè wasn't getting me anywhere. I was trying to be my own person, but first I had to find myself.

Chapter 6 – Derek

The crew was pissed about what happened to me at the mall. I told them not to sweat it because none of Tamika's girls could fight. Hell I got jumped by three girls and didn't have one bruise on my face. Takia's wild cat fighting skills were no match to my blows. I probably hurt the three of them more than they hurt me.

A week went by and there was no sign of Takia. We walked up and down her street everyday after school hoping to catch her sleeping. It got old after a while but Shavon wasn't ready to let it go.

I still had my job at Shoe Express but I carried a shank that Trè gave me for protection.

On one of my off days I decided to stay home and spend some time with Sharod. I was reading him one of his children's books when I heard someone knocking. I gave the book to Sharod and told him that I would be right back. I looked through the peep hole to see who was knocking and was surprised to see it was Shavon. I opened the door and noticed her shady facial expression almost as if she was hiding something.

"Come in, what's up with you?" I opened the door to let her in. I couldn't help but wonder why she stopped by unannounced. The girls would usually call to see if I was home before they stopped by.

"Nothing's up, you busy? I gotta show you something."

"I was just reading Sharod a book, what's up?"

She walked down the hall and went straight into my room. I followed behind her after telling Sharod I would be right back.

We were both standing inside my room looking at each other.

"Shut the door T," Shavon said.

I shut the door and sat on the bed eagerly anticipating for Shavon to show me whatever it was that had her popping up at my crib. She pulled up her shirt and pulled out a 9mm gun that she had tucked in her pants.

"Girl look at this, I just brought it off Taqwon."

I looked at her like she was crazy. "Shavon, what the fuck do we need a gun for?"

"Shit, you never know when the next time you may see one of them bitches, you got a knife, but they probably have one too. We need this T."

I knew that Shavon came over to get my approval and my gut told me to tell her to sell it back to Taqwon or someone else. Instead, I told her to put it up just in case we needed it.

The next day I had to go straight to work after school. That morning I straightened my hair so that it fell on my back, then I curled my bangs and swooped them over my eyes. The length of my hair made it look like a weave, but it was all natural.

Work was boring as usual especially after my ex-friend the cashier quit. I was pretty sure she never wanted to run into me again, which was very smart because I would have probably whooped her ass every time I saw her.

I was leaning against the counter when this brown skin attractive dude with a fresh low fade and a body that looked as if he went to the gym on a regular approached me. He had the sexiest lips I had ever seen and I tried not to drool as I looked him up and down. I had to check out his outfit. He had on a fresh white T-shirt with new tan Timberland boots, a B-hat, baggy jeans that didn't sag too low and a gold chain with a big ass medallion. Mmm, he looked delicious.

"What's your name Ma?" he asked approaching me at the cash register.

"It ain't Ma," I said giving him attitude with a flirty smile.

"My fault, can I get your name?" He grinned. I noticed that he had a chipped tooth like the rapper Nas, but it was sexy to me.

"My name is Tiara, what's yours?" I couldn't believe that I was actually flirting back. I usually gunned dudes down that tried to talk to me in the mall, but there was something about him. The fact that he was gorgeous and had a gangster swagger that made me weak to my knees may have had something to do with it.

"My name is Derek."

I was so glad I decided to put the time in to do my hair before work. I usually rocked it in a ponytail like a damn hoodrat in case I ran into some chicks that I had beef with. But today I looked just as fly as Derek did in my uniform.

I extended my hand to shake his. "Nice to meet you Derek."

We exchanged numbers and I went home that night floating on air.

When I got home I couldn't wait to call Tamika and I had her call Renée on her three-way. They could tell that I wasn't acting like the usual laid back Tiara. I was bubbly and so anxious to tell them about Derek. I mean, I had male friends but that's all they were, I wasn't interested in any of them because I was too picky.

"Okay, tell me why I met the finest dude in the mall today? See, I told y'all to come up there more often."

"He got any friends?" Tamika quickly asked.

"Girl I don't know but if so you know you got that, I'll hook you up."

"Girl, what about me?" Renée asked.

"I'll hook you up too, but shit can I see if he's even worth my time?"

"Well you said he was fine, that's enough to earn your time. Does he look like he got money?" Renée asked.

"Hell yeah, he had on a big ass gold chain and his gear was on point."

Tamika got excited. "Oh word! Then you know you gotta see what up for me, I need a baller in my life."

Renée chimed in. "Hell yeah, I need a nigga to keep me looking fly."

"Wait T, what's his name and where's he from?" Tamika asked.

"His name is Derek, I don't know what block he's from yet. I'm gonna call him but you know I gotta play it cool and act like I'm not interested."

My other line beeped.

"Hold on y'all somebody's on my other line." I clicked over. "Hello?"

I heard an unfamiliar deep voice. "Hello can I speak to Tiara?"

I got butterflies in my stomach because I knew this wasn't one of my homeboys, his deep voice sounded like a mellow Barry White but with a hood appeal. Since I didn't have a positive male role model in my life, I always compared guys to Trè. He had to be gangsta, he had to be real, he couldn't be a cornball that got chumped by his friends, he had to be leader and I was hoping that that's what I would find in Derek.

I finally answered Derek trying to hide my excitement. "This is Tiara, can you hold on for a second?" I bit my bottom lip.

"A'ight beautiful," Derek said. He had me even more open than he did at the mall.

I clicked back over with the biggest smile on my face and I took a deep breath. Tamika and Renée were still chatting it up. "Sorry y'all, I'm gonna have to talk to y'all bitches later, this is Derek."

"Yo, see if he has any friends," Tamika pleaded.

"Alright Tamika damn, I said I got you, I'ma call y'all back later."

I quickly disconnected them and got back to Derek. "Hello?" I blushed, batting my eyes like a shy child.

Derek's sexy voice replied, "Hey beautiful, I'm glad I caught you at the crib, what you doing? I know you must be tired."

"I'm just sitting here chillin' and watching TV, what you doing?" I lied to Derek, I wasn't watching TV but he didn't need to know that.

"I'm chillin', I'm at the studio in Roxbury."

"Oh so you rap?"

"Something like that, you ever heard of The Hustlers Camp?"

"Yeah, they performed at the Strand Theater in Dorchester a few weeks ago."

"Yeah that's us, those are my niggas."

The Hustlers Camp was a local rap group in Boston. They created a buzz by doing shows and radio appearances. Everybody in Boston knew who they were and I was talking to the sexiest one. I couldn't wait to tell my girls about this.

"What are you doing this weekend, do you have to work?" Derek asked.

"I work on Saturday from eleven to five, why what's up?"

"Why don't you and some of your girls come to my boy's house to chill after you get off, he's having a get together? Plus you and I can get to know each other."

I tried to act disinterested. "I'll think about it," I said teasing him.

"I want to see you, don't do me like that," he playfully whined.

"I'm just playing, where is it?" I asked.

"It's the brown house on the corner of Dudley Street in Roxbury."

"Alright, we'll be there around 8 o'clock."

"I look forward to it."

"Me too," I said smiling like I was going on a date with Denzel Washington.

"I'll call you tomorrow, aight?" he asked.

I smiled even bigger. "Alright."

I hung up the phone picturing how sexy Derek looked at the mall earlier. I had to call the girls back to let them know everything.

I called Tamika, she called Renée on her three-way again and they wanted to know it all.

"So does he have any friends?" Tamika asked.

I laughed. "Bitch if you ask me that shit one more time…"

"My fault T, I'm excited like I'm the one that met the nigga. What y'all talk about?"

"Well he invited us to come to a get together on Dudley Street this weekend. Oh and guess what?

He rolls with The Hustlers Camp so y'all know we gotta go looking extra fly."

Renée got excited, "Now that's what I'm talking about, y'all know we gotta hit up the mall right? Oh and Tiara can I borrow your black heels?"

I rolled my eyes. "Yes Renée you can rock them AGAIN. This time take care of my shit."

"You got that girl thank you."

Working at Shoe Express helped me to acquire a wardrobe. I didn't mind letting my girls use anything, they were like my sisters. If I loved you, what's mine was yours. Renée was good for asking to borrow my stuff. She thought she was super diva or some shit.

The weekend rolled around, I got off work at five and headed home to get dressed. I was on some different shit; I wore a tight low-cut fitted pink shirt that showed the D-cups I normally hid in girlie fitted t-shirt tops. I was showing enough cleavage to make a baby's mouth water. I put on some eyeliner and lip gloss to enhance my already pretty face. My hair was hanging down my back and I swooped my bangs over to the side. I definitely looked fly, Beyoncè had nothing on me.

I never thought about how we were actually getting to the get together. Karen came down to my apartment when she was done getting ready. We had told Shavon, Ke-Ke and Karen about Derek and his boys and they were just as excited to go as Renée and Tamika.

"Karen, how we getting there? I damn sure ain't getting on no bus."

"Shit, I thought they were picking us up."

"Nah, I didn't ask him to pick us up and I don't feel like paying for no cab either."

The phone rung and it was Tamika calling. "Yo T, we'll be there in five minutes so come to the front of the building. She hung up the phone quick. I didn't know what the fuck these bitches were up to but I knew it had to be something crazy. Karen and I grabbed our purses and we headed to the front of the building and walked outside.

Five minutes later Shavon, Renée, Tamika and Ke-Ke pulled up in an old Jeep Cherokee. I walked up to the driver's side where Shavon was sitting.

"Bitch, who's fuckin' truck is this?"

Shavon smiled bobbing her head to Tupac's Hail Mary. "Just get in y'all, we got some wheels for the day."

I booted Tamika out of the front passenger seat, Karen got in the back and we were out.

I didn't ask anymore questions about the car on the way to the get together because we were having too much fun. We knew all the words to every song on Tupac's album and we were cruising through the city streets like we owned them.

We pulled up to Dudley Street and Shavon parked the car. I waited for the girls to get out of the backseat because I wanted to talk to Shavon. Shavon was about to open her door when I grabbed her arm.

"Listen Shavon, you better not be up to no shit."

"Chill T, I borrowed this car from Taqwon."

I crossed my arms. "What's up with you and Taqwon lately? I hope you ain't fuckin' him."

She gave me a sly smile. "Now T, you know Trè wouldn't let his boy bang his little sister's homegirl."

"Why the fuck not? You got ass and titties and he's a dude."

"Chill T for real, it's cool, now let's just go have fun."

I took Shavon's word for it and we all headed towards the brown house. I rang the doorbell hoping that someone would hurry up and open the door because it was chilly outside. This dark skin grimey looking fat dude answered the door.

"Is Derek here?" I asked, looking past him hoping to see Derek.

"Come on in, everyone is back there in that room over there." He pointed and opened the door wide for us to come in. Ke-Ke was the last one to come in and as he closed the door I caught him looking at her figure.

"Mmm," he said sounding like a thirsty ass nigga.

Ke-Ke blurted out a loud "Ugh!"

I grabbed her and whispered. "Ke-Ke chill, don't even trip, let's just have fun." I always had to be the one to keep the crew under control like I was their mom.

I opened the door to a smoky large master bedroom where everyone was drinking, smoking weed and listening to beats. I spotted Derek next to one of his friends writing some rhymes. I wanted to melt right in his arms. He looked just as sexy as he did that day in the mall. He looked up and saw me enter the room and walked over to me.

"You were beautiful the first day I saw you but DAMN!" He smiled.

I laughed and started blushing. I was definitely happy he was feeling my appearance.

I turned to my girls. "These are my girls Ke-Ke, Renée, Shavon, Karen and Tamika, y'all this is Derek." They all looked him up and down and gave me a look of approval.

We looked around and noticed that we were the only girls there. I guess it was good just in case they invited some chicks there that we didn't get along with.

Derek's friend Moe turned down the music. "Yo D, you invited the head bus'ers?"

We all frowned up our faces wondering what the hell he was talking about. Karen rolled her eyes like dice, I could tell she wanted to unleash the bitch and cuss Moe out.

Derek responded. "The head bus'ers? Nigga what the fuck are you talking about?"

Moe held his hands out in front of him. "Chill, they be bus'in heads, fuckin' bitches up." He looked at all of us shaking his head up and down. "Yeeeeah, I heard about y'all." He noticed our faces started to relax. "Chill, it ain't nothing bad, I just heard that y'all don't take no shit."

The girls started to ease their attitudes and I even cracked a smile.

"Yeah that's us," Ke-Ke said sounding like she wanted a hoodrat of the year award.

Moe looked Ke-Ke up and down. "I see you boo." He turned the music back up and took Ke-Ke's hand and led her to a seat next to his.

While Ke-Ke and Moe were chatting, Derek asked the other girls if they wanted a drink. Everyone asked for beers and he brought back some Corona's popping the tops off for us.

Derek had a few more cute friends besides Moe and they were mingling with my girls keeping them occupied. Derek took my hand and led me into a quiet corner in another room so that we could talk without the music interrupting us.

"I'm really feeling you Tiara," he said.

I smiled, "I'm feeling you too, well from what I'm seeing so far, you're mad cool."

There was an awkward silence and I nervously looked around not knowing what to say next.

"Why you sitting so far away from me Tiara, come here?"

I was a little reluctant but I scooted my chair over next to his. He grabbed my hand, "You're gonna be my little shorty, watch."

Shavon came out of the smoky room with the ugly fat dude that answered the door for us earlier. "Oh there you are T, I'm about to take a ride with him real quick and smoke this blizz. I was pissed, her body language showed that she was acting out of character; she was falling on this dude and didn't even know him.

"Bitch, you don't even smoke and you're drunk, how many beers did you have?"

"Chill T, we'll be right back, I had like three beers, I'm a little nice but I'm straight."

"Come right back," I said pointing my finger to the floor.

She stumbled out the door falling on Derek's fat ass friend slurring. "A'ight T, I'll see you in a second." I was pissed off because Shavon was acting like a hot mess.

Derek looked over at me. "Damn, calm down, my man ain't gonna hurt your girl."

"Yeah I know that, it ain't him I'm worried about, it's her."

Derek grabbed my hand. "The only thing you need to be worried about is me and you."

He managed to crack the hard shell that I had just formed and I was blushing again. We spent the whole night talking and getting to know each other. He was a good listener, he wanted to know everything about me and I opened up to him because he made me feel really comfortable.

Two hours had gone by and Shavon still hadn't come back and needless to say I was heated. The girls were ready to leave and that's when my anger turned into worry. The phone rung, Derek's friend picked it up.

He shouted out to Derek, "Yo this is Big Man, he said they got arrested."

"What! For what?" Derek yelled back.

His friend put the phone back up to his ear to get more answers, he shouted back out to Derek, "He said a stolen car and a hammer."

Derek yelled out to his friend, "Why the fuck did he ride in the car with her with the hammer on him."

"It wasn't on him, it was on her, chick was packing a 9mm."

I closed my eyes and wanted to melt in the floor from embarrassment.

Chapter 7 – He Say, She Say

I was so mad at Shavon, I didn't even want to visit her. I tried not to let my anger get the best of me so I swallowed my pride and visited her on the Monday after the weekend. I hadn't called or spoken to Derek since the get together because I was too embarrassed. I knew he probably thought we were some hoodrats that carried guns and acted a fool.

I took a long bus and train ride to visit Shavon. I waited in the visiting room ready to let her have it. She came walking towards me, her hair was in sloppy cornrows that she put in herself. I gave her a hug, asked her how she was and then laid it out.

"Shavon, for some reason I knew some stupid shit was going to happen when you left with that boy."

She shook her head. "T please, don't come up here preaching, I got enough shit on my plate right now."

"Shavon, why the fuck was you carrying the toast? I told you to put it up for a rainy day and you were out here rocking it like a damn bra. Not only that, you didn't tell me the fuckin' car was stolen and I kept asking you about it, you could've got us all locked up."

Shavon gave me a serious look. "T, I'm serious, my bail is twenty grand and my grandmother won't accept any of my phone calls and I'm facing a two and a half year bid.

I calmed down because I could see that she was really going through it. "If I had the money I would have bailed you out with no questions asked, you already know that. You're my dog and whatever the outcome is, I'll be on the outs doing this time with you. I got you on your canteen money, I'll be frequent on the visits and I'll even visit your grandmother for you."

The worry in her face eased a bit. "That's some real shit T, I really don't have anyone but you." Tears formed in Shavon's eyes but she quickly tried to wipe them, this was the first time I had seen her cry, it was weird because I was used to her being so tough. "Tell the girls to hold it down out there, I love them to death but I know them ho's won't be coming up here often."

"Don't even worry about none of that, focus on you, read, write, and do whatever you have to do to pass the time but I'm here for you in or out."

She looked me in my eyes. "That's the realest shit I've ever heard."

"Girl please, you been real with me from day one Shavon, I'm returning the favor, stay up a'ight, DPG for life."

We both stood to our feet and hugged each other just before the visit ended and we parted ways.

When I got home I noticed that my mom was past out on the couch next to an empty wine bottle. Sharod was running around the house unsupervised having the time of his life. I took Sharod in the bathroom and bathed him. I fixed him a sandwich and then I put him down for bed.

I went back in the living room to wake up my mom. "Ma, come on, let me take you to your bed."

She tossed and turned and then slightly opened her eyes. "Oh hey Tiara." Her words were badly slurred.

"Ma, you're drunk, you finished the whole bottle knowing that Sharod was here, you gotta slow down with this drinking."

"Taqwon," my mom blurted out.

"Ma, what are you talking about? You're talking in your sleep."

She repeated it again, "Taqwon!"

"Ma, what about Taqwon?"

"He's dead."

"What do you mean Taqwon's dead Ma, where's Trè?"

My mom started crying. "I don't know Tiara, I don't know, find my son please Tiara." She turned over and laid in the wet pillow full of tears.

"I'll be right back Ma." I rushed out the door.

Taqwon was Trè's ace and I knew that whoever killed him would be getting killed next and so did my mom. I knew that she was also worried that Trè could be getting killed next. Trè's crew was grimy but they hadn't killed anyone yet, well as far as I knew.

I headed straight to Trè's block, there were like thirty dudes on the street, some were in tears but they wore the coldest faces full of anger and revenge.

"Where's Trè?" I asked one of the dudes on the street. He pointed up the block and I spotted Trè. He was with like six or seven dudes talking in the cut. I walked up to Trè and pulled him aside.

"Trè, I'm sorry about Taqwon, do you know what happened?"

Tears were in Trè's eyes. "These bitch ass niggas that we fucked up caught him sleeping without his toast earlier today. You already know what it is T, it's on." Trè looked to see who was coming up the street in a random car. "T, I want you to go home, it's hot around here a'ight."

"A'ight Trè, be careful, make sure y'all get them niggas, do it for Taqwon, but make sure you be safe a'ight?" I gave Trè a hug, I knew that he was hurt, whenever Trè was hurt, I was hurt plus Taqwon was my homey too, he was like another brother.

On my way home, I thought about how Trè said Taqwon had got caught without his toast. I wondered if Taqwon had got caught sleeping because he sold his gun to Shavon. I know Taqwon wasn't stupid enough to sell his toast to Shavon without having another one for himself, plus Trè had plenty to give him. I didn't know what to think and shit was getting real stressful.

I got home and called Tamika, her voice was full of sympathy. "We heard about what happened to Taqwon on the news, that shit is fucked up, how's Trè doing?"

"He's a'ight, mom dukes is stressing though, she's drinking like crazy worrying about Trè. I hope they catch those niggas though."

"You know Trè and them are gonna catch them, they are no joke, but the crew was reminiscing about Taqwon, that was our nigga, this shit is crazy."

"I know life is short and fucked up. I don't wanna lose anyone else to the streets. We have to live every day to the fullest because you never know what could happen." I said.

"Girl you are right about that."

"A'ight, I'm going to bed, I'm tired and this has not been my week. I love you girl I'll see you tomorrow."

"Love you too, good night."

As soon as I hung up with Tamika my phone rang. I picked it up with an attitude.

"Hello!" I was tired, stressed and just wanted to go to sleep and you can hear it all in my tone.

There was silence before someone asked, "Can I speak to Tiara please?"

"Who's calling?"

"It's Derek."

I relaxed my tone, "Hey Derek, what's up?"

"Damn, I didn't know who that was picking up the phone like that."

"I'm sorry, I got a lot on my mind, one of my homeboys just got killed and you already know the deal with Shavon."

"I'm sorry to hear that. Why haven't you been calling me? I could be your shoulder to lean on, I told you that you were gonna be my little shorty."

"Derek honestly I don't know if this would work. The first day I chill with you, my girl gets locked up with your boy. Moe was basically calling us hoodrats talking about we be bus'in heads and the whole night was just fucked up."

Derek laughed. "Tiara, this is the hood, shit happens all the time, you can't blame yourself for shit that happens around you. It's not your fault that your homeboy got killed or that Shavon and my boy got locked up."

"I know Derek but it just seems like shit keeps happening to me, I just want to be happy, I want all my people to be happy."

"Let me take you out tomorrow after school, you need to get away, I guarantee I can make you smile."

"Don't be fresh Derek."

He laughed. "No I ain't talking about sex, I'm serious, I'm going to put a smile on your face, I promise."

"Alright," I agreed.

I hung up the phone with Derek and without him even knowing, he had already put a smile on my face.

I went to sleep with a clear mind that night erasing out all the bullshit and looked forward to my day with Derek.

The bell rung, last period was over and all of the students rushed to the door for dismissal. I met up with Tamika in the front lobby and we headed for the door to go home. When we walked outside, I heard this car bumping some familiar music that I had heard on our local radio station Jammin' 94.5 FM. It was one of The Hustlers Camp's hottest tracks.

"Girl is that Derek?" Tamika asked.

My eyes focused on this dude leaning against a white Honda Civic. "Yeah that is him, come on."

Tamika and I walked over towards Derek. I stood right in front of him looking him in his face.

"Is that a smile I see?" he asked.

I couldn't hide it and my smile grew bigger. He opened his arms to hug me and I gladly embraced him. His cologne invaded my senses making me want to drink it off his neck. His muscular frame made me feel safe, I felt like I was hugging my soul mate. When we finished hugging, I had to shake off the lust and stay focused. And of course I had to look out for my homegirl, "Derek, do you mind giving Tamika a ride home too?"

"No problem, she lives around your way?"

"Yeah, I'll tell you how to get there."

When we were in Derek's car, we looked out the window and saw so many groupie ass chickenheads from my school staring us down. This chick Shareka and her girls in particular were staring a hole through the car.

"Tamika, you see this shit?"

"Yeah these bitches are hating, that ain't anything new, I just laugh at these fake ass hoes because they know if we stepped out of this car them bitches would plead the fifth."

We both laughed.

"Look at y'all starting trouble," Derek teased as he pulled off.

"We ain't starting trouble, we're good girls, and trouble finds us."

"That ain't what I heard," he said.

"What did you hear?" Tamika asked sitting up closer to us from the back seat.

"I'm just playing, chill; I don't want y'all to bust my head."

I looked at him and hit him on his arm. "Oh you got jokes huh?"

Derek laughed.

Before we got to Tamika's house, I noticed Trè and his friend Terrance walking up her street. I tried to turn my head so that he wouldn't notice me. Derek peeped me trying to hide my face. "What, did you see one of your boyfriend's or something?"

"No smart ass, I saw my brother Trè, you know how dudes get when it comes to their younger sisters."

Derek tried to drive and look back at the same time. "Oh, that was Trè back there? That's your brother? He's a real ass nigga. He fuck with my older cousins, they are mad cool."

I felt a weight lift off my chest, it felt good knowing that Trè didn't have beef with anyone that Derek knew, if so, things would have eventually gotten ugly.

Normally, if any of my male friends came over to the building to chill with me and the crew and Trè was home, he would either rob them or check their nuts. He made so many dudes seem like cornballs because they were so scared of retaliating because they knew how Trè's crew got down. Some dudes wouldn't even approach me because of the fact that I was Trè's sister.

We parked in front of Tamika's crib and she stayed seated like she didn't want to get out of the car.

Derek and I gave her a look that let her know her time was up.

"Bye y'all have fun," she said being sarcastic.

I got an instant attitude. "What's wrong with you Tamika?"

"Nothing, just have fun call me later."

I could tell that she was being sarcastic but I didn't want to go off on her in front of Derek. She never liked when I did things without her. Sometimes she acted like I was fucking her or something. When she finally got out the car, Derek pulled off.

"What was that about?" he asked.

"My cousin Tamika is like that sometimes, she always wants me to put her first like I can't have a life without her.

"Well she's gonna have to fall back because you're going to be with me more often from now on."

Derek drove down to the Charles River in Cambridge. We walked around the water talking and holding hands. I felt like I was in a romance novel. I felt so free away from the hood.

The water was so peaceful and the reflection of the city lights off the buildings made the scenery more romantic.

"Derek, I really appreciate this, I needed to get away and just be in a total different environment for a little while."

He stopped walking and pulled me close to him. "I plan on having many more days like these with you." He pulled me even closer and pressed his soft lips on mine. I closed my eyes and indulged in his sweet kiss. He gently sucked my bottom lip into his mouth and I softly did the same to him. We kissed passionately for what felt like forever as I melted into his arms. My panties were getting wet and I felt his manhood rise. That's when I pulled back, I didn't want him thinking that things would go any further than that.

I was the only one left out of my girls that was still a virgin because I admired the fact that my mom married her first love and I wanted to do the same. I knew I didn't want an asshole like my father, Orlando or Primo, I wanted to take my time and make the right choice when it came to who I was giving myself to. I wasn't just going to let anyone have my goodies like my girls had done. They were very free with their bodies.

Derek was very respectful and didn't say anything when I pulled away from him. We just continued to walk until we had circled the entire river.

He took me home around ten o'clock and we shared another passionate kiss in the car before parting ways.

As I was exiting the car, Derek grabbed my arm. "Tiara, I want you to officially be my shorty? I want you to be my girl."

I paused for a moment faking the funk like there was something to think about, I knew I wanted him to be mine and only mine, I looked in his chocolate brown eyes and responded, "Yes."

He put his hand on his heart. "You done made a nigga's night."

I smiled. "You're a mess Derek, call me when you get home." I walked to the front door of my building. He made sure that I had the door open and was inside before he pulled off.

Derek was officially my boyfriend. This was new to me, I had male friends, hell I had even kissed and been fingered before but it never went beyond that. I didn't trust guys at all. I used to think that every dude would be like my father if I let them get too close. So once I had any type of feelings for anyone, I would cut them off. It was different with Derek, I guess I was just getting older and more open for love.

Almost everyday Derek would bring me lunch at work, and he always picked Tamika and me up from school. I was officially spoiled and I could see that Tamika was becoming more jealous than happy for me but I brushed it off.

Derek was taking me to see Shavon on the weekends and when I turned seventeen and entered my senior year in High school he taught me how to drive. I got my license and then it was a wrap. He would let me use his car and my girls and I would go tear up the city. I had to include the girls in my time every so often because they felt like I was dissing them for Derek.

I was officially in love with Derek. He was perfect, a thug yet a gentlemen and I felt like he was my savior from the hood. For the first time in a long time, I was happy and Derek gave me something to look forward to.

131

Ke-Ke and Moe also remained together so I would see her most out of the crew because we used to chill at the studio with the other girlfriends of the Hustlers camp.

Ke-Ke and Moe actually made a cute couple. For the first time, someone was taming Mrs. Hoodrat into a lady. Every time I saw her and Moe together, I could see that she was glowing and Moe loved to floss her around town. She had a killer body and the sexual escapades that Ke-Ke would tell me about them two were like some porno shit. I didn't have any sexual stories to exchange with her yet because Derek was actually being patient with me.

Derek and I were doing well until Tamika called me on some other shit. "Tiara, remember them bitches that were grilling us the first time Derek came and picked us up from school?"

"Yeah, Sha- Shareka I think her name is, her and her girls, why?"

"Well I found out that they were starring us down like that because Shareka used to fuck with Derek and I hear they are still fuckin'."

I laid back and tried to digest what my girl had just told me. "Hold up Tamika, who told you this shit?"

"One of her girls told me yesterday, so you know I had to tell you."

"A'ight, good looking out, I'm about to call his ass right now."

I hung up with Tamika and called Derek so fast that I hit the wrong buttons. I had to redial it and I was becoming impatient with the phone ringing. I wanted him to hurry up and pick up so that I can rip him a new ass hole. As soon as I heard him say hello I immediately started ripping on him. "So you're fuckin Shareka?" I caught him off guard, he didn't know what to think or say.

"Who?"

"You know who I'm talking about, the bitch from my school!"

"Oooh that bitch? T calm down, I used to talk to her last year. It ain't that serious, she's a slut bucket, I only hit it once and that was it, I don't respect bitches like her plus I didn't even know you at the time."

"So why the fuck am I hearing that you're still fuckin' her?"

Derek let out a sigh. "Somebody's lying to you, I wouldn't do that to you, that chick been off my list."

"Yeah whatever."

I hung up with Derek and immediately called Tamika back because I needed to find out more information.

"Tamika, what's the bitch's name that told you this?"

She sounded a bit funny and unsure. "Um, I forgot, but it starts with a K, I think her name is Kim."

"Well I just asked Derek about it and he said whoever said that is lying."

"Well T you know how niggas lie."

"Yeah but it's all good, I'll see that bitch Shareka at school tomorrow."

I woke up early the next day to get ready for school because I couldn't wait to confront Shareka. As soon as school was over, I was dog checkin' that bitch. I couldn't understand how the fuck she could see me in school everyday smile in my face and fuck my dude behind my back. I definitely had it in for that bitch.

Last period seemed to drag on forever and when the bell had finally rang I rushed to the front door waiting at the top of the stairs until I spotted Shareka. I saw her in her usual spot waiting for the rest of her girls to meet her. "Shareka, what's up with you and Derek? Y'all still fuckin'?" I asked getting right to the point.

"Nah that was just a one day thing, Derek's a dog, well he dogged me," she said.

I got in her face. "So why is your homegirl telling my girl that y'all are still fuckin'?"

Tamika came walking towards us which was perfect timing, I was hoping that she would point out the girl in Shareka's crew that told her about this.

"I don't know what you're talking about," Shareka said dumbfounded.

I looked over at Tamika. "Tamika which one of these bitches behind Shareka told you that shit about Derek?"

Shareka's girls knew how my crew got down, they didn't even react to the fact that I just disrespected them all, when I got mad I didn't give a fuck and everyone knew that about me.

Tamika looked behind Shareka as if she didn't see the girl and she didn't say a word.

I turned back around to continue confronting Shareka. "Well who is Kim?"

I wanted to get down to it and find out who was this mysterious Kim chick that told Tamika about this.

"I don't even have a friend named Kim," Shareka said.

I turned and looked at Tamika with a strange look on my face, I was confused and then I became embarrassed so I took it out on Shareka.

I knocked her in the face with my backpack and we began exchanging punches. Her girls didn't even jump in. They just sat there watching as I whooped her ass. Tamika eventually jumped in and when we got her on the ground and started kicking her I screamed, "Bitch, if I ever hear about you even looking at Derek, I'm gonna fuck you up again!"

After the fight, I couldn't help but wonder if I beat up Shareka for no reason. She basically told me the same thing that Derek told me, that it was only a one time thing. But why would Tamika lie to me? The shit just didn't make sense.

When I got home I called Derek and told him that I beat his little girlfriend's ass. He just laughed and told me that I was crazy.

I wanted to take my mind off of the situation so I decided to spend some time with Sharod. I took him to a park next to Trè's block, it was the only park that we had around so I still took him there despite the neighborhood.

I was talking with Sharod while pushing him on one of the swings at the park.

"My friends at school usually have their fathers or big brothers picking them up after school. Sometimes Ma comes to pick me up drunk and I keep trying to tell her that drinking isn't good for her," Sharod said.

My heart broke and I was crushed. I knew that was a cry for help. He wished that he had a father figure to step up in his life. Orlando moved on with his life and only called for Sharod on Christmas or birthdays. He was an official dead beat dad. Trè was too busy running the streets. The only relationship he had with our six year old brother was showing him how to fight or showing him new guns that he purchased off the streets. No one was around to teach him how to be a man or to raise him properly. I knew I had to step up.

When we passed by Trè's block on the way home, I noticed a ton of police cars on the street. I saw a bunch of Trè's friends against a fence being searched and then handcuffed. I happened to look further down the street and noticed that one of the dudes was Trè. I turned Sharod's body around so that he wouldn't see our big brother going to jail.

"Damn!" I said. I began rushing Sharod home.

When I got home I tried to let a few hours go by before calling to see what precinct Trè was booked at. I found out that he was being held at the jail in Dorchester. They told me that he was being charged with possession of marijuana and a firearm. Trè and his boys got caught up while trying to get revenge on the dudes that killed Taqwon. When they got back to their block, they were searched and brought in.

Trè's bail was set at $15,000 and I knew there was no way I could get that kind of money from anywhere. If I could've got the money, I would have bailed him out and not told my mom about it. But now I was forced to tell her.

I walked into her room, she was watching TV, and I couldn't tell if she was sober or not because she started to wear the alcohol look more than the sober look a bit too much lately.

"Ma, Trè just got locked up. They said that he had some weed and a gun on him."

She got up off her bed and headed for the vodka bottle on her dresser. She picked up a tall glass and filled it to the top. "Tiara, nothing surprises me from Trè anymore."

Tears started falling from her eyes as she put the cup up to her mouth about to take a sip. "Tiara, get out, I want to be alone right now, just go."

I turned around to leave her room and noticed that Sharod's head was peeping in the door. He tried to scurry to his room when I saw him. I followed behind him to explain the situation because I knew how much he adored Trè.

He was lying on his bed and I rubbed his little back. "Sharod, everything is going to be alright trust me. I promise you that big sis is going to take care of everything. Trè's going to be gone for a little while but if you need anything, you let me know okay?"

He sniffed and wiped his eyes. "Okay."

I got in the bed next to him and slept there that night, I just wanted Sharod to be comforted because my mom was going downhill and I was all that he had.

Chapter 8 – Friends

It was prom night and my mom finally felt like she had something to look forward to. Trè never made it to his prom because he had dropped out years ago, so she felt like this was a major accomplishment for me.

After long aggravating drawn out court appearances, Trè was sentenced to three years in jail. My mom and I showed up at each court date and I made sure that I was frequent on his visits just like I was with Shavon's.

As we waited for Derek to pick me up, my mom snapped picture after picture. "You look so beautiful Tiara." She stood looking at me smiling.

Sharod was watching all of the excitement as we waited for Derek as well. "Yeah sis, you look like a superstar."

Derek knocked on the door, I rushed in my room to get my purse and my mom opened to the door to let him in. "Derek, you're a fine young man, make sure you take care of my baby tonight and y'all have a good time." I kissed my mom and Sharod and I headed outside.

Derek had rented a Corvette, it was off the chain. It had leather interior and it was fast as shit. He was still selling drugs so he made sure that he balled out on me. When we arrived to the prom I felt like Cinderella arm and arm with my Prince. I was the flyest chick there and Derek was the flyest dude there. Tamika and I spotted each other and hugged like we hadn't seen each other in years. Tamika was still single so she came to the prom with her older cousin Jerome.

"You look too good girl," Tamika said checking my dress out from top to bottom.

I turned around to model my backless champagne colored dress. "Thank you, you look fly too."

Tamika turned to look at Derek. "Hey Derek," she said as if she didn't want to speak, she was still stuck on him being this dog that Shareka's so-called girl Kim said he was. She never let the situation go but I didn't give a fuck, he was my man and I stuck by him.

The DJ played hip-hop all night and Derek and I danced the night away. At the end of the night the DJ started playing slow jams. I couldn't believe the school let him play R. Kelly's "Bump N' Grind". Derek and I bumped and grinded on each other as if we were making the video for R. Kelly. I felt his manhood stiffen as I grinded my ass further and further into his crotch, I wasn't holding back.

After the prom Derek told me that he had plans for us. He pulled up in the parking lot of the Ramada. "T, I got a room reserved in here for us, but I don't want to pressure you, we're only gonna go in here if you're ready."

I knew that I had deprived Derek for too long and it was time for me to give ALL of me to him. Trè always told me that if a man waited for me for at least a year, then he's not only there for sex but he's there for me and Derek waited for almost a year. Normally I wouldn't let him get further than sucking on my titties but tonight was our night. I knew that he would be my future husband and I didn't want anybody else but him, he was my all.

I was scared out of my mind but I was also excited. "Yes, I'm ready Derek."

He parked the Corvette and we headed into the hotel lobby. Derek had already made the reservations and had no problem checking us in. We took the elevator up to the hotel room and my heart was beating so fast, I could feel it pounding in my ears.

Derek opened the hotel door, I flicked on the lights but they were set to dim. I looked around and noticed Derek had the whole room decorated with red rose pedals leading to the bed. It was beautiful and romantic. He had fresh strawberries and whipped cream on the night stand with a bottle of Moet and two champagne glasses. He made sure that my first time was going to be special.

"This is beautiful Derek, I only see luxury shit like this in the movies." I sat back on the bed to take everything in.

Derek sat down next to me. "Tiara, just remember, we don't have to do nothing you don't want to do." He was such a gentlemen but I knew that he wanted to dig in my draws just as much as I wanted to give it to him.

I embraced Derek hugging him tightly so that he could feel my appreciation. Then our lips found their way to each other and we began tonguing each other down aggressively. Derek stood up and went over to his boom box that he had brought to the hotel earlier. He pressed play and R. Kelly's mixed CD was perfect for the setting.

He met me back at the bed and we began kissing again. He slowly laid me down on my back as we kissed, one of his hands caressing my breast, the other hand trying to unzip my dress. His sexy muscular body was grinding on me making my juices flow like rain. He stood to his feet to take off his suit, stripping down to his boxers. Through them

I could see his dick readily standing at attention. I was a little taken aback at the thought of taking all of him inside of me.

I couldn't believe this was really happening. I stood up so that Derek could help me completely take off my dress and before I knew it I had nothing on but my panties and bra.

Derek laid me down and he looked as sexy as a paid male model. He reached for the strawberries and whipped cream. He sprayed some whipped cream on his finger, placed it in my mouth and let me suck it off.

He had a hard time undoing my bra so I quickly helped him and tossed it to the floor. Then he spread whipped cream on both of my nipples rubbing it in with his fingers before sucking it off as if he were being breastfed.

He nibbled on my nipples and used gentle circular motions with his tongue and then took his fingers to massage my kitty through my panties.

After taking his time enjoying dessert off my D-cups, he placed a strawberry in my belly button and gently ate it off like it was the best thing he had ever eaten. His tongue made its way down to my virgin kitty and nibbled on it through my panties. I was so wet and turned on that I didn't know what to do. He finally removed my panties to give me complete and total satisfaction. He French kissed my kitty for like an hour giving me my first long overdue orgasm.

My kitty was extremely wet and I knew that he would have no problems sliding his dick inside me. He stood to take his boxers off and then laid on top of me, I was scared shitless. It was finally about to happen. Seeing his manhood through his boxers was nothing in comparison to the real thing. His shit was large and I started to get scared. He reached over for the condom on the nightstand and rolled it on. I reached over to pour myself a glass of Moet and downed the whole glass.

Derek laid on top of me kissing me passionately, he lifted his head to my ear and whispered, "Are you ready?"

I closed my eyes tight and whispered, "Yes."

At that moment, I felt the head trying to penetrate me as he spread my legs apart. I kept pushing my body back until my head hit the headboard as he tried to push it in more and more. I couldn't believe that people actually enjoyed sex, it was painful!

He was finally able to get it all the way in, he stroked slow and gentle. "Are you okay?"

I nodded my head up and down. After a while the pain subsided and it started to feel good. I still couldn't believe I was actually having sex, something that my girls had been doing for years. I was fortunate to give myself to someone who loved and respected me and I had no regrets. He was my man and my future husband.

The next morning Derek took me home and I was immediately interrogated by my mom. "Why is your hair messed up? Where did you sleep last night?"

"Ma, we went to a get together after the prom and I fell asleep there."

My mom looked at me with a face that told me she knew I was lying. "I ain't stupid, anyway, you got a letter on your bed from your brother."

Trè and I kept in touch with each other throughout his whole bid. But people that I loved knew that I was always the one to count on. I would give Shavon and Trè canteen money before I would go get some new shoes and I loved dressing up for Derek, but I didn't mind.

I started reading the letter from Trè and he put all this bull crap in it about how when he get out he was gonna change. I didn't believe that for nothing.

I decided that I was going to take Derek to meet Trè. My mom and Sharod adored him and I knew that it would make me feel good if Derek and Trè became friends.

When we got up to the jail, I could tell that Derek was nervous to meet Trè but he put on a front and handled himself well. He was meeting someone who he had heard so much about through his cousins as well as other people on the street and most of what he heard wasn't good. I felt like I was taking Derek to meet my father. For some reason I just always wanted Trè's approval. Trè arrived in the waiting room and it was a contact visit so we didn't have to sit behind a glass.

"Derek this is my brother Trè, Trè this is Derek."

They both nodded their heads up at each other saying what's up.

"I seen you from somewhere before," Trè said looking at Derek.

"Yeah, I roll with The Hustlers Camp and you be with my older cousins Jeff, Bronson and them."

Trè smiled "Oh a'ight, those are my niggas, those are your cousins? Tell those niggas I said what's up."

The ice had been broken and Trè and Derek were talking as if I wasn't there. I was happy like a fat kid with cake, Derek was officially in good with my family.

When Derek and I got back in the car to go home, he kept telling me how cool my brother was. Derek's family was cool with me as well. He was an only child and his mom was the sweetest lady that I've ever met. I knew that I wanted a long future with Derek so I wanted to talk to him about living right so that we would be straight in the future, too many people were getting killed and I didn't want anything to happen to him.

"Derek, eventually I want you to get something legal, this drug shit is too overwhelming, I mean the money is good but I worry about you all the time."

He parked in front of my building and turned my face to look in my eyes. "Don't worry about me baby, I'm yours forever. Eventually I'll give this shit up, but I don't be out here wilding out like some of these niggas. I do my little bit of hustling and I'm in the studio, I ain't about that trying to be tough shit."

"I know baby but niggas be jealous when they see another nigga shining," I stopped with that thought. "I've seen it happen before."

"T, don't worry about none of that, I ain't going nowhere. I'm gonna keep stacking until I got enough to get us both out of here, until then, I'm always on the low."

I gave Derek a peck on the lips and I went in the house. Things with Derek were so perfect, I still managed to see the girls as much as possible even though Derek and I were inseparable. It wasn't until I got some disturbing news from a phone call from Ke-Ke that fucked up my whole vibe.

"Tiara, you're my dog and when some disloyal shit happens amongst the crew, I wouldn't be real if I didn't let you know."

"What are you talking about Ke-Ke, let it out?"

She took a deep breath and hesitated, I could tell that she didn't want to tell me whatever it was.

"A'ight fuck it, I'm going to tell you everything. Okay, remember a while ago when

Tamika told you that Derek was still fucking
Shareka?"

"Yeah the bitch that Tamika and me fucked
up at my school."

"Yeah her. Well Tamika told me that she
made the whole thing up. There was never a girl
named Kim and she just told you that because she
knew that Derek fucked Shareka before so the story
seemed more believable if she told you that they
were still fucking. I don't know what's up with her
lately T, she been talking real greasy about you on
some hater shit."

My head was spinning beyond control.

"That sneaky bitch! Are you fuckin' serious
Ke-Ke?"

"Yeah T for real, and that ain't the worst of
it, T before I tell you this just promise you won't do
nothing stupid?"

I got agitated with Ke-Ke. "Ke-Ke, stop
stalling and tell me what the fuck you have to say."

"Alright T. She's fuckin' Derek. He parked
his car at Moe's crib and got in the car with us and

Moe dropped his trifling ass off at Tamika's. He always parks his car at Moe's crib in case you ever went to Tamika's house and saw his car out there. He's trying to be smart about the shit nigga."

My heart fell out of my body and I lost all control over myself.

"Ke-Ke, tell me you're joking, this is a joke right?" I knew Tamika was sneaky and low down in some ways but I would never in a million years expect this from her.

"T, on some real shit, I wish I could tell you this was a joke. I didn't want to get in the middle of this, but you're my muthafuckin nigga and that's supposed to be your cousin that shit is more than grimy."

I tried to collect myself. "Well, you already know what's about to happen."

"What you gonna do T? Don't do nothing stupid, just cut both of them off."

"Oh, I'm gonna cut them off, but first I got some shit to handle right now."

Chapter 9 - When It Rains It Pours

My mind was going a hundred miles per minute. I was gonna kill that bitch. I called a cab hoping to get to Tamika's before Derek had time to leave. A million thoughts were crossing my mind. She must have fucked him after I told her how big his dick was. All the private shit I shared with Tamika that I didn't even tell the other girls she used against me. We were supposed to be family.

The cab pulled up to Tamika's house, I hopped out and headed straight up her stairs to the front door. I turned to look at this car speeding down the street stopping in front of Tamika's house. It was Moe and Ke-Ke, I figured that she must have

156

told Moe that she told me about the situation and Ke-Ke knew that Tamika's would be my first stop.

When Moe got out the car, I ran down Tamika's stairs to confront him before knocking on her door. "What the fuck are you doing here? You were dropping your boy off over here knowing that I'm his girl, knowing this shit is foul?"

Moe shook his head, "Tiara I don't want to get in the middle of this shit, Derek is his own man, I have nothing to do with this situation, and I'm just here because my girl wanted to check up on you."

"Whatever Moe, all niggas stick up for each other, you're probably a dog ass nigga too."

I turned to run back on the stairs and I knocked. I heard Tamika's voice.

"Who is it?"

I put on a fake voice. "It's Ke-Ke."

She opened the door shocked to see me outside. "T, what you doing here?" Her presence disgusted me, I didn't even let her finish talking, I just struck her in the face with my fist with all my might. She was taken completely by surprise. I took her by her hair and dragged her down her stairs. I was fucking her up, after each blow I was screaming at her. "You lying trifling bitch! You like being a ho? I'm gonna show you what I think about ho's." I drug her over to a pile of dirt on the sidewalk and smashed her head all in it. "That's what I think of you, you dirty bitch!"

Derek watched from a window until he gained enough courage to come outside. He ran over to me. "T are you crazy, what are you doing?"

Ke-Ke tried to get me off of Tamika, Derek pushed her out of the way grabbing me and then pinning me up to Moe's car by my collar. "Calm down T, I ain't fuckin' her." I went wild like a chicken with its head cut off trying to break away from Derek's hold on me.

"Get off me you liar, you're fucking fake Derek, everything we had was a lie! Get off of me, let me finish fuckin' that bitch up!"

The scene was so dramatic, the neighbors started to look out of their windows and some even came on their porches to watch.

Ke-Ke began crying. "We are girls, we are bigger than this shit, and we don't need to be fighting over no nigga."

"That ain't my fuckin girl, she ain't shit to me!" I said still going wild.

Tamika finally managed to get off the ground and decided to be bold. "Fuck it let her go Derek." She looked at him and then looked at me. "Look at the nigga you let come between us T, I just fucked him to let you know that he was a dog and no nigga is worth you putting me to the side."

"That's the best you could come up with bitch? That you fucked him to show me he is a dog? Derek let me go, let me get at this bitch!" I grabbed his hands trying to break loose.

Tamika began to get really brave. "Let her go Derek, she wanna get at me over some dick then let's get down."

"Oh so you're tough now bitch, I just whopped your ass, you didn't get enough?" I spat.

Ke-Ke's eyes were pouring with tears, she knew that this meant a big part of the crew was going to be broken up, Tamika and I were the bread and butter of the crew, the bitch was suppose to be my damn cousin.

"Please stop y'all, fuck that nigga, Tiara if he fucked her he ain't worth it and Tamika you know you're fucked up for this!"

Tamika rolled her eyes at Ke-Ke while she spoke, she knew she was wrong but began being defensive, "Fuck both of y'all, I'm good on y'all."

"Fuck us? Nigga, you're the one that put yourself in this predicament, fuck you!" Ke-Ke looked at Tamika as if she was about to fight her next.

While they began arguing, Derek managed to pull me inside of Moe's car. "T, let me talk to you, calm down please, it's not that serious."

I frowned up my eyebrows looking at him like he was crazy. "Fuckin' someone who I consider my family isn't that serious Derek?" I shook my head and smacked the dog shit out of him. "It's over! If you see me on the street, don't even look my way."

I turned to get out of the car, he had one hand up holding the cheek that I just reddened and he started pleading. "T, I'm sorry, she threw the pussy at me, and I was stupid. I admit I fucked up. I can't lose you T, not over this, not over some bitch that wasn't real with you from the beginning."

I just looked back at him, I had no words for him. I opened the door to get out of Moe's car and started attacking Tamika again while she and Ke-Ke argued.

I snatched her up. "Oh so you thought this shit was over bitch!"

Tamika and I had been fighting with other chicks since we were young, even before we formed the crew, now that she wasn't off guard I knew she would put up a good fight. But my anger took over and once again I had this bitch on the ground. This time I was stomping her until I became exhausted. I was huffing and puffing while she was blocking her face trying to avoid another kick. I stepped back and conjured some spit inside of my mouth and as she unblocked her face, I spit a mouth full right in her grill. "You're dead to me bitch!" I turned to look at Ke-Ke, Derek and Moe. They were staring at me like I was crazy.

I turned and started walking down the street and none of them came after me because my body language showed them that I didn't want to be bothered.

I cried all the way home, I needed the time to myself. I thought about everything that Derek and I had shared, how much he taught me about love and how he said that he would eventually give up the game so that we could have a future together somewhere else. Everything seemed like a lie now, I gave my all to him and in return I got played by him and with someone that I considered my family. Tamika and I had so much history together and she knew everything about me. Sometimes your best friend could be your worst enemy. My head was all fucked up, I had lost two people that I loved and would give my life for, all in one night.

When I got home my mom walked towards me with money in her hand, she wanted me to see if one of the neighbors could go to the liquor store for her. She looked a little closer at me and noticed that my eyes were still moist from crying, she grabbed my face turning it side to side looking at the fresh scratches and then at my wrinkled collar from Derek holding me.

"What's going on Tiara, you out there fighting again? It better not be that boy putting his hands on you."

I looked at my mom, I couldn't hold my tears back, and I put my face in my hands and started balling. Usually, I would hide my drama from my mom because she did enough worrying about Trè, but this time I couldn't help it.

"Mom, hug me please." I wanted to feel her love. I wanted to feel like someone cared about me who was sincere. I was the one caring about everyone else and the backstabbers in my life weren't appreciating it. My mom embraced me and I cried on her shoulder.

"Whatever it is Tiara, let it go, it's not worth it. Nobody in this world is worth your tears. Give your burdens to God and don't let anyone on this earth take away your faith."

I sniffed and then tried to talk through my tears. "Ma, why do things keep happening to me? I'm a good friend, I try to be a good person, why do I blame myself for everything and why does it seem like everyone around me let's me down?" I was hoping that my mom had the answers to all of my questions.

"Baby, God gave you the strength of a million men and you have a heart of gold. I feel like I failed you as a mom but even with you seeing my weaknesses, you're still striving for better. I always told you don't be like me, be better than me and I see better in you everyday. You can't let the lives of others interfere with your journey."

Those were the wisest words I had ever heard my mom speak. I was going to keep on keeping on and do me.

After trying to put all that drama behind me, I couldn't help but to think about Derek because he was calling me constantly everyday up until my graduation. I tried to stay focused at school and concentrate on graduating. Tamika managed not to look me in my eyes when we saw each other at school after the incident. I couldn't lie, if she ever looked my way after all that went down, I still had a fresh ass whooping on call ready for her bitch ass.

Graduation came and went and I was accepted into a community college. I tried to stay focused to pursue a better life for myself. I was ready for my transformation into a woman. It was time to leave that juvenile stuff behind. Sometimes it takes some fucked up shit to happen to you to make you realize that things had to change.

I stopped chilling hard with the crew even though Karen, Ke-Ke and Renée would pop up to tell me the latest gossip on the streets. It was all getting old to me. I still visited Shavon and when I told her about Tamika she wasn't surprised. She said, "I knew she was a fake bitch, she was always mad that she couldn't have you to herself, that shit was scary sometimes, fuck that ho and I better not catch her when I get out."

After what Tamika did, the whole crew considered her an enemy but it was only a matter of time that I would run into her again.

It was the last day of college before Christmas break and, I couldn't wait to get home. I headed to the train station dreading it like I did everyday. I never realized how spoiled I had been from driving Derek's car and I hated trains ever since. I quit my job at Shoe Express so that I could focus on college so I knew that I was going home to either sleep or to chill with Sharod. Before I approached the train station I saw four girls with scarves on. I had too much pride to try to take another route to the station so I continued to walk towards the girls. I knew that it was either some girls that I had beef with or some chicks looking to rob someone because that was the only time that my crew wore scarves. As I got closer to the girls, I noticed some familiar faces. It was Takia, Monique, some non-descript bitch and the fourth girl was none other than Tamika.

It was all starting to make sense. Tamika always missed the brawls that we got into with Takia and her girls so they had no problems accepting her shady ass to be down with them. Plus she knew everything about us so that was a benefit for them. Our moms were still close and I'm pretty sure that's how Tamika found out what college I went to and told them, so I was being set up. They were all grilling me as I got closer and I boldly looked them all up and down, "What is this Sluts R Us?"

"For a bitch rolling by herself, you got a lot of mouth," Takia said.

"You should know me by now Takia, whatever's whatever." I looked over at Tamika but kept talking to Takia. "I'm sure your new crew member told you how real shit is over here."

As I was talking, Monique circled around me trying to find an angle to come at me. I followed her with my eyes trying to make sure I was on point if she tried something. It was hard for me to keep control of what all four girls were doing. Monique finally caught me from behind and started pulling my hair. I couldn't believe these bitches felt that they had an advantage over me and for the first time they were actually letting me have it. If it wasn't for the non-descript chick, I probably could have handled it better but that bitch was big. She was actually bigger than Shavon. I tried to go toe to toe with her but if it wasn't for Takia and Monique trying to release years of anger from me whooping their ass over and over, I probably could have done some damage to the chick. Tamika managed to get a hit in but for the most part she watched. She wanted revenge after I beat her ass and embarrassed her but she knew deep down that she deserved it, that's why she eventually broke it up.

"A'ight y'all, chill." Tamika said after about fifteen minutes of scuffling.

Everybody backed up, but my adrenaline was still racing. "So y'all bitches want to jump me, let me handle all of y'all one by one!"

Someone had told the train attendant inside of the station about the fight and they called security and we heard it over the intercom. Takia and them ran while I gathered myself to go home and strategize on how I was going to get my revenge.

When I got home I called Karen, she called Ke-Ke and Ke-Ke called Renée and before long we were all on the phone together. Their blood boiled after I told them what happened to me.

"That bitch is chilling with who?" Karen asked in disbelief.

"Yes girl, she's chilling with Takia and them now." I said.

"You know what T, we got this and you don't even have to get your hands dirty even though I know you want to, but fuck it, we will handle this," Ke-Ke said.

"Hell yeah!" Renée and Karen said at the same time.

Renée sighed, "Damn, after all these years of us being a crew, who would have thought that Tamika would switch dicks and roll with Takia and them; who we have been banging with for years."

"Yo Renée, just from you saying Tamika's name again got me wanting to go and beat her ass again."

"Nah T, we are going to handle this, she betrayed you and now the bitch is chilling with our enemies, I'm about to wrap up my weave as we speak and meet the crew around Takia's way, it's on and poppin'."

Later on that night, the girls came over to my building and we talked in the hallway. They were all holding their stomach's cracking up laughing.

I was smiling looking at everyone. "What's so funny," I asked.

"Yo, tell me why we caught your girl Tamika coming out of Takia's house, we ran her for all her shit, and then made that bitch strip butt naked and walk home."

I giggled. "Y'all are lying!"

"On dog's nigga, we made that bitch strip! She had no problem showing niggas her goodies before so we made an example out of that bitch," Ke-Ke said screwing her face up.

I grinned, "That's what the fuck she gets, and shit for old time sake we should rob Takia again."

"I'm down!" Ke-Ke said.

I knew they would all be down but I had to think about what I just said; I was supposed to be moving forward not backwards.

"On some real shit y'all, if shit pops off, then no doubt we'll handle it, from now on let's leave the hoodrat shit to the little girls and try to get our grown woman on.

"Ah T you getting soft on us," Karen teased.

"Nah, never that boo, I'm on some grown woman shit, and it's time for us to focus our energy on making some real money."

Ke-Ke lifted her head up and batted her eyes. "Well until then, I'll stick to Moe, my money maker."

"Oh boy," Karen said rolling her eyes.

"Don't hate, but I have to go home and get dressed, me and Moe are going to the movies tonight after he drops off Derek."

I looked at Ke-Ke and paused, "Now you know not to mention that nigga's name in my presence."

She put her arm around me. "I'm sorry T, my fault. But I'm off this, I gotta go get pretty."

The girls left the building and I went back into my apartment and laid on the couch. I knew that what I had told the girls went in one ear and out the other. They were living for today, none of them focused on the future like I did, I felt them because of their circumstances but I wanted more than living in the hood, I had Sharod looking up to me, my mom was drunk everyday, Trè was still incarcerated and there just had to be a light at the end of the tunnel.

I fell asleep on the couch but was awaken a little while later by a knock on my apartment door.

I rubbed my eyes. "Who is it?"

I heard a familiar voice but I knew it couldn't be. I opened the door and it was Derek. He looked terrible, his eyes were bloodshot red and I could tell that he had been crying.

"Derek what are you doing here, is everything okay?" I pulled the door up behind me and stepped into the hallway.

He took a deep breath and then became hysterical as he began speaking, "I needed to see you, some shit just went down." He was pacing back and forth in the hallway talking dramatically with his hands.

"What happened?" I knew that it was serious, men didn't just cry for anything.

"One of our deals went bad and some niggas just tried to rob me and Moe, we made it to the whip, we were bursting our hammers back and forth with the dudes." Tears began streaming down his eyes. "Derek calm down, look at me, where's Moe?"

Derek looked at me, his eyes sad like a starving puppy. "He's dead."

Chapter 10 – I Forgive You

I couldn't believe that Moe was dead. I embraced Derek holding him tight not letting his betrayal block my emotions.

"I'm so sorry Derek." I began to cry with him.

He let go of me grabbing me by my waist and looked at me. "T, you were right, I needed to get out of this game. Niggas got us twisted because we rap, they think we got money like that. We are on the same level as the next nigga hustling."

"Do y'all know exactly who did it?"

Derek looked at me, his face full of vengeance. "T, they took Moe, they took Moe!" I knew he didn't want to tell me that he knew exactly who took Moe because I knew whoever had done it would be getting taken out. Derek started banging on the walls in the hallway of my building.

"Derek calm down, the neighbors are going to come out, come over here."

He came walking towards me and put his back against the wall then squatted and placed his face in his hands. "They took my man T, my man is gone."

He couldn't preserve the tears that he had inside his tough interior, he started balling out of control, crying like he had a body part cut off. I never heard a man cry that loud, but this was death and Derek was hurting.

I consoled Derek but I also knew that I had to console my girl. I knew that Ke-Ke would be a mess once she found out about Moe. "Derek listen, give me the keys to your car, we have to go tell Ke-Ke about Moe, I'll drive."

He handed me the keys without saying a word. Ke-Ke lived down the street in the projects so I didn't have enough time to prepare how to bring the news to her. We approached the projects within ten minutes and I walked to Ke-Ke's apartment on the first floor and took a deep breath before knocking on the door. Derek stayed in the car staring at the dashboard totally in shock.

I knocked on the door and Ke-Ke answered the door in tears. Someone had already told her the news.

"T, my man is gone, somebody took my baby."

I grabbed Ke-Ke and held her tight. "We gotta be strong okay, I'm here for you no matter what, we are gonna get through this okay?"

Derek came walking through the hallway, when Ke-Ke saw him she demanded answers. "Derek who did this? Who took Moe?" She continued crying and yelling not letting him get a word in edge wise. "How could y'all let him die Derek, Moe is gone, I can't believe this!"

Derek just shook his head. It was obvious he didn't know what to say to her. Her mom heard her crying loudly in the hallway and came to her side, she looked at us. "I got her, I'm going to bring her back in the house and try to calm her down," she said. "She'll be okay."

"Ke-Ke I'm going to keep calling to check up on you okay?" I told her.

Her mother took her into the house and Derek and I headed back to the car. During the ride I was watching Derek's body language and he kept fidgeting. I could tell that he was in deep thought. His face read guilt and he couldn't handle it.

"T, I feel like this is all my fault. If I never lost you, my man would probably be here right now. You kept me off the streets, and when I lost you, I ain't gonna lie, I was out here doing some grimy shit because I felt like I had nothing to lose. Now I lost my man and none of this shit was worth it. I fucked up, I fucked up bad."

"Derek, you can't blame yourself—"

"But I feel like it's my fault T, I can't bring my man back." He turned to look out the window.

"Yeah but you can live for him, the old Tiara would have told you to go ride out on the

178

niggas that did this, but the new me is focused on life, on living for the future."

Derek grabbed my hand. "I need you T, just be here for me through this, please."

We approached my building and I pulled up to the front. "Derek, I have always been a loyal person, I will be your friend through this but we will never get back what we had."

A disappointed look came across his face. "That's good enough for me."

I gave him a hug to show him that I would be his shoulder to lean on and I left to go into my building.

A week later, we buried Moe. It was the week before Christmas and everyone was still in mourning. I still loved and cared for Derek and secretly wanted to be with him, but after he did the ultimate no-no, I knew that we could never be.

I was there for Derek through all of his grieving and I also tried to be there for Ke-Ke. The Hustlers Camp had decided to put recording on hold until everyone got their minds right regarding the

Moe situation. Derek came and picked me up everyday that week and we would just talk about what we wanted out of life and I tried to keep his mind busy because he was still blaming himself for Moe.

The holiday season was extremely stressful. My mom started drinking even more because she knew that she couldn't afford the toys that Sharod wanted for Christmas. I was out of work so things really didn't look too good for us.

Even though I felt like shit, I decorated the tree with Sharod knowing that it would be basically empty underneath. He was still excited about Christmas and it tore up my soul to know that I couldn't get him anything.

Christmas Eve approached, the only toys that we had under the tree were toys from Globe Santa. Globe Santa were toys given to the parents who couldn't afford to give their kids Christmas gifts. Sharod was so sweet, he knew our situation, he told my mom that whatever he got he'd be satisfied and that he understood. He was a smart boy, he reminded me of myself because he had to grow up fast because of the lifestyle that he was forced to endure. I just hoped that things like this wouldn't spark him to want to get money the fast way like Trè did once he hit a certain age. I made a vow to myself that I would not let Sharod be a statistic to the streets.

Derek called around noon and I was glad because I had to vent out to someone, I felt useless and ashamed that I couldn't provide for my little brother.

"Derek, this shit is really fucked up, my little brother is smiling and has the Christmas spirit but his Christmas is not going to be anything special."

"Tiara, you know Sharod is my little man. I refuse to let him have a fucked up Christmas, I'm going to go out and get something for him, for you and your mom."

"Derek, I wasn't telling you for you to feel sorry for me, I just wanted you to listen."

"T, I got you, I'm doing this for y'all, if I didn't fuck up with you that would have been my future little brother."

"Don't start Derek." I rolled my eyes and looked at the phone. "Seriously, don't worry about us Derek, I'm looking for a receptionist job and I'll be able to hold my family down soon. Usually Trè holds us down for Christmas and I did what I could when I was working. This time, we'll just look at Christmas as another day."

Derek didn't give up. "Well you still haven't convinced me not to look out for y'all, I owe you way more than this T. I'll call you when I come from the mall so that I can swing through and drop off the gifts."

"A'ight Derek, but don't over do it." I was about to hang up when I heard Derek call my name.

I put the phone back to my ear. "I'm here."

"I'm really sorry about hurting you and I want to know if you could forgive me. You don't have to answer me now. But losing Moe made me realize how precious life is. I let my selfishness and weakness break your heart and I feel fucked up for it. I wish I could turn back the hands of time but I can't, so your forgiveness would ease a burden on a niggas heart. Now I know you might be thinking that a nigga is soft but I got feelings too. I love you and I hope one day we could start over a'ight?"

My heart melted, I wanted to reach through the phone and kiss Derek's soft lips, I wanted to embrace him and tell him that I forgave him and that I loved him and missed him more than words could express. But I knew that I couldn't, I just couldn't let him win after what he had done to me. Tears began falling from my eyes as he spoke and I had to put the phone away from my ear to sniff so that Derek wouldn't know that I was crying.

I cleared my throat. "Derek, we can talk later, I'll see you when you come back from the mall okay?"

"Okay my sunshine, I miss what we had T, just think about forgiving me."

Derek and I hung up and I headed into the kitchen to help my mom with Christmas dinner.

Sharod and I baked some cookies and I was actually getting into the spirit. I thought about what Derek had just said to me and how good of a heart he had to really make Sharod's Christmas worth remembering. Derek had money so I knew that whatever he got for Sharod would be something that he would like and I couldn't wait to surprise him.

An hour later, out of nowhere, things changed.

Knock! Knock! Knock!

I heard an obnoxious banging on my apartment door. It seemed as if the door was about to cave in. I opened the door only to find my cousin Tamika in tears. I could barely understand what she was saying.

"Come in, what's wrong?"

"T, it's Derek!"

I tried to calm her down. "What do you mean it's Derek?"

"He just got shot!" Tamika cried.

I felt my head spin. "Who told you this? Are you sure it's Derek, *my* Derek?"

"Yes Tiara, your Derek," she insisted. "He was rushed to the hospital and it ain't looking good T."

I began sobbing uncontrollably. All I could do was drop to my knees and pray. It couldn't be Derek, not my first love. I had just talked to him an hour ago!

It was Christmas Eve and he told me he was going to the mall to shop for last minute gifts. I just knew that my prayers would change the news that Tamika had just told me.

My mom came in when she heard us crying and tried to calm us down. She kept saying how there must've been some sort of mistake, but there wasn't.

I was shocked to see Tamika at my crib but I was glad that someone told me before I heard about it on the news. We quickly rushed outside, Tamika had some dudes car and I just hopped in with her, no questions asked. I prayed the whole way to the hospital. It was the most painful ride of my life. I had so many questions. I just couldn't believe this was happening.

When we arrived at the hospital, I left Tamika outside and I burst through the emergency double doors and screamed at the receptionist. "I need to see Derek Nelson!"

The receptionist looked at me puzzled, I could tell that she didn't know what to say.

Bitch why are you just staring at me, I wanna see Derek fuckin' Nelson!"

"Ma'am, you're going to have to calm down."

At that moment, Derek's mom came out of the doors behind the receptionist desk. I ran over to her. "Ms. Nelson, is Derek okay, what room is he in?"

She looked up at me and her face already told me what she was about to say. "He's gone Tiara."

I was in denial, "Where did he go Ms. Nelson, did he go home?"

"No Tiara, he's gone."

"I just spoke to him an hour ago, I want to see him! I don't believe you." I put my hand on my head, everything felt like a bad dream to me, I knew that I would wake up at any minute.

She grabbed both of my arms and tried to keep me from pacing. "Tiara, listen to me, Derek didn't make it."

I wasn't taking her word for it. "You're lying Ms. Nelson I don't believe you, he's okay, please tell me that Derek's okay."

Ms. Nelson was crying, "I can't tell you that Tiara, my baby didn't make it, he got shot four times in the chest."

She became hysterical and started screaming at the top of her lungs. She no longer cared about convincing me about Derek, she was feeling her own pain as she took a step and past out.

Several nurses ran to catch her and rushed her into one of the hospital rooms.

A few of Derek's friends from The Hustler's Camp entered the hospital and everything became a blur to me after that. They were asking me questions but I couldn't hear them. I just knew that Derek had to be okay, there was no Hustler's Camp without Derek or Moe. Seeing them in the hospital with two missing links made things seem more real to me.

"T, please tell me Derek's okay," Derek's friend J.B. asked.

I turned to look at him trying to understand what he had just asked. I couldn't focus. I felt like I was under water. I heard a nurse call my name, "Is your name Tiara?" I shook my head yes. "Ms. Nelson wants to see you, can you follow me please?"

Without speaking, I followed the nurse into the room that they had Ms. Nelson lying in. She was sitting up on the bed and had calmed down and wanted to talk. "Tiara, come here sweetie."

I walked over and sat on the side of the hospital bed. "We have to face this situation because it's the only way to bring closure."

"What do you mean?" I asked.

"I want you to come with me to see Derek, you have to see him or else you won't be able to put a reality to this situation." Ms. Nelson put both of her hands on top of her long mane and grabbed two handfuls.

When she let go of her hair, she stood up, grabbed my hand and said, "Let's go say good-bye to my baby."

I felt the emptiness of her broken heart by the hold she had on my hand. Her hands were shaking and her eyes were full of tears. Derek was Ms. Nelson's only child and her husband had died when Derek was only nine years old. Derek was all that she had.

Nothing could prepare me for what I was about to see. We entered the cold room and I saw Derek lying lifeless on the hospital bed. My eyes bucked wide in shock, I put both of my hands over my mouth. It was true, someone really had taken Derek's life. I had to compose myself, plus I didn't want to lose it any more than I already had in front of Ms. Nelson. I conjured up enough courage to walk over to Derek to touch him. I rubbed his cool forehead.

I bent over to whisper in his ear, "Save a spot for me in Heaven."

I stood up straight and stared at the first and only man that I'd ever loved. I looked over at Ms. Nelson, she didn't make it as far as I had, she couldn't bring herself far enough to touch him, she ran out of the room crying, my heart shattered for her. I looked back down at Derek, his eyes were still opened wide like he was in shock when he died. Tears and snots strolled down my face and I didn't bother to wipe them. I noticed that the doctors tried to hide the tubes that were stuck in his chest as well as the blood that was on his body. They had a white sheet covering his stomach area but I was still able to see that Derek had lost a whole lot of blood plus he still had blood spats on his cheeks. I didn't care, I still leaned over to lay a kiss on his cheek, this was the last time that I would see Derek and in my heart I felt like he was still listening. One of the nurses came in the room and told me that I had to leave. I leaned over Derek, shut his eyes with my two fingers and then bent to whisper in his ear again, "You're at peace now, I forgive you."

I gave him one last long and final kiss on his lips, they were cold and stiff and didn't feel the same but I closed my eyes and imagined that he was kissing me back. I headed for the door but first turned around to take a final glance at my first love and I blew him a kiss. I couldn't believe that this had happened to me. I was prepared to tell Derek that I forgave him after he came from the mall. Some coward took his life before I got a chance to reveal to him my forgiveness. It was too late for me to let Derek know how much I still loved and cared for him. It was painful to leave him so I turned back around and went back to his bedside and I kissed him again, this time my tears landed on his face and I spoke my final words to Derek, "Merry Christmas my first love."

I walked out of the hospital room leaving my heart on the hospital bed with him.

Chapter 11 – My New Friend

I was depressed for years after losing Derek. Before I knew it I was twenty-three years old, still living at home with my mom and I couldn't keep a job because I couldn't focus. I blamed myself for losing Derek. Word had it, Derek lost his life retaliating for Moe. On his way to the mall, he saw some niggas from the same block that killed Moe, he pulled out his hammer, started thumping at the dudes when a car full of their boys were behind Derek and lit his car up. I blamed myself because I felt like I could have stopped Derek from going to the mall, after all, he was going for me.

Ke-Ke handled Moe's death differently. She tried to get over Moe by dating mad dudes and not getting attached. She went through about four guys, all notorious drug dealers using them for their money, jewelry and whatever else she could get out of them. She figured that if she didn't let her feelings get attached then if anything happened to the dude, she couldn't get her heart broken again. She looked at all guys as objects and she was getting hers. I even let her crazy ass convince me to go out with one of the top drug dealers in Boston. I had nothing to lose, Sharod was thirteen and I felt like I had failed him as a sister. He knew that I couldn't keep a job and the little money that I made while I was working went on him, but of course it wasn't enough.

My mom was now a full blown alcoholic and Trè got out of jail, but it wasn't long before he was locked down again. I was all Sharod had so I figured that by dating this drug dealer, I'd be able to provide a better life for Sharod without him knowing where the money was coming from. I wasn't in it for feelings, I tried to keep my game face on and do this for my little bro.

Shavon had been out of jail for a few years, she found out that her grandmother had passed away while she was locked up. Throughout Shavon's entire bid, despite all the bullshit that I went through while she was locked up, I was still by her side the entire time. I scraped money for her canteen and as much as I hated riding the bus and train, I did it to be there for my girl when no one else cared if she was alive. It goes to show how some people whom you consider your friends could give two fucks about your loyalty. Come to find out, her grandmother left her pretty well off. When she got out of jail she came home, took her money and moved with her sister to Texas.

All of the time and money that I spent on Shavon was in vain. I should have let her fat ass rot. The little money that I spent on her could have been spent on Sharod. She didn't even stop by before she moved. Word on the streets was that she tried to move before people could start asking for hand-outs. I felt like Shavon and Tamika had both failed the crew in their own way. Tamika thought she

194

could weasel her way back into my life after the Derek incident. I kindly thanked her for delivering the news to me about Derek but told her as far as our friendship went, she could suck my dick if I had one.

Renée, Ke-Ke, Karen and I were now closer than ever. I guess throughout the years we had to separate the real from the fake but it hurt like a bad tooth ache. Tamika and Shavon were my dogs, we been through it all together, for the two of them to burn me the way that they did made me feel like all friends should be kept at a distance. But the definition of being real to me is looking out for your people by any means necessary and I was still loyal to Renée, Ke-Ke and Karen.

The night that Ke-Ke took me to meet my new friend the drug dealer was exciting, yet I was nervous. It's been so long since I had talked to a dude on that level, I didn't even know what I was going to say once I met him.

My new friend's cousin Shawn was one of Ke-Ke's many men, she came and scooped me up in his car, a Mercedes Benz 500. We were rolling in style in the big body Benz on twenty-two's. I got in the car and looked around at the flawless gray leather and suede on the seats, the TV in the dash board and the two screens behind the headrest and tried to soak it all in.

Ke-Ke turned down the music, "See girl, I be rolling in cars like this on the reg. Just think his cousin has more money than him. You lucky I didn't meet him first."

"Ke-Ke you're crazy." We both laughed. "Ke-Ke on some real shit, he don't have no drama with him right? No baby momma's, no mistresses and shit?"

"Not that I know of but if so fuck it, you ain't in it for love, get yours T, if you don't the next bitch will."

I turned to look at Ke-Ke while she drove. This was a total different Ke-Ke. "Bitch, you are really on some fuck niggas shit! You don't have feelings for at least one of these niggas you fuck with?"

Ke-Ke twisted her lips. "Hell no and I'm not about to start. Life is too short and their money is too long so I would like to continue to get my piece. Cha-ching!" Ke-Ke formed her fingers like she was thumbing through money.

"You're crazy as shit. You better be careful doing this." I turned and looked out of my window. "I can't believe you got my ass out here like a damn gold digger, we are supposed to be better than this Ke-Ke, but we are still out here in our twenties like some damn hoodrats using niggas."

Ke-Ke pulled over to the curb in front of these stairs that led to a beautiful mansion on top of a hill. "Who deserves it more than us T? We been through some shit, it's time for us to live."

"Why haven't you hooked Renée or Karen up yet?"

"T, these are high-end niggas and you know Renée's chickenhead ass wouldn't know how to act in front of them and Karen's attitude isn't built for these niggas. I know how you are, you can adapt to any situation, plus like I said, no one deserves this more than us."

I got distracted as I looked out at the beautiful mansion that was secluded from other homes; it looked like a house in Beverly Hills. The kind of houses that you saw in movies. Milton was a town in Boston where a lot of rich white people lived and if a black person was able to afford a home in Milton, then they had to be twirkin with some serious dough.

Ke-Ke scraped the rim on the Benz trying to park closer to the curb. "Oops my bad, he'll be a'ight, he got enough money to fix it," Ke-Ke said.

I shook my head, "Bitch you are out of control."

We got out of the car and headed for the stairs. We had to climb about twenty stairs to get to the top. The house was a beautiful colonial style house that looked like it had about thirteen bedrooms. It had a double garage but the lot was full of cars that looked like they were never driven and I could see why Ke-Ke parked on the side of the street because there was no room in the lot. Ke-Ke rang the door bell, she fixed her hair while we waited tucking her new long weave over to one side behind her diamond studded ears. Ke-Ke was literally laced from head to toe. I on the other hand had on an old outfit, no jewelry, and nothing special, just natural beauty. If we didn't click, then it wasn't meant to be.

Ke-Ke's friend Shawn answered the door. "It's about time, you must have been out joy riding in my shit again." He looked over at me. "How you doing?"

"I'm good" I said.

"Tiara, this is Shawn, Shawn this is my girl Tiara."

I nodded my head at Shawn. "Nice to meet you."

He looked me up and down like he was examining each part of me for his boy. "Yeah, Tony's gonna like that."

Shawn appeared very cocky to me.

"Where is he Shawn? Tell your boy to come down here so he can meet my girl. I need you to take me to get some money, I'm getting my hair done tomorrow and I seen this new bag that I wanted in Copley."

I looked at Ke-Ke, I gave her the screw face that she usually wore and I thought to myself, "If this bitch leaves me here with this nigga by myself, I'm gonna fuck her up."

Shawn yelled up the spiral staircase for his friend to come downstairs.

"Yo Tony, come down here man, they're here."

I looked up the stairs, I couldn't wait to see what the infamous Tony looked like. He stood at the top of the stairs looking over the banister before walking down the stairs. He walked up to me with a blunt in his hands rolling up some weed.

While licking the blunt, he looked me up and down. "Damn, Ke-Ke said you were pretty but you're a dime piece."

"Nice to meet you too," I said.

He finished rolling his blunt and put it on a nearby table. "My fault boo." He extended his hand to greet me. "Nice to meet you Tiara, I'm Tony, T-Money."

I reached for his hand and he grabbed me close and hugged me. "I don't shake hands boo, this is how you greet me."

He was just as cocky as Shawn. I got a good glimpse of Tony for myself. He was gorgeous, if he was a chick, he would've been a dime piece. He was at least six foot one, a solid hundred and seventy pounds, light brown puppy dog eyes and long fresh groomed braids. His skin was like dark chocolate and it was flawless, not one pimple was on his face. He had his hair lined up and he looked good enough to eat, the fact that he had a lot of money made him even more attractive.

Ke-Ke grabbed Shawn's hand. "Well we are gonna leave y'all to get to know each other."

I rushed over to her. "Where you going, you ain't leaving me here?"

"Chill Ma, my man ain't gonna bite you," Shawn said.

I shot him a look that told him to mind his business. "Well I don't know your man so I'm good, I'm not staying here by myself."

"T, I won't be more than 15-30 minutes, it's cool, and these are my people."

I finally let my guard down. "A'ight, hurry up Ke-Ke."

When Ke-Ke and Shawn left, I turned to look at Tony, he was smiling. I could tell he knew that I felt awkward but he told me that he thought it was cute. I didn't trust anyone especially after Derek died, it was hard for me to be around anyone that I didn't know.

Tony started walking, "Come on into the living room." I followed behind him. He led me to his butter soft white leather sofa. His living room was decorated with Al Pacino pictures from the Scarface movie. He had a 52-inch plasma screen hanging from the ceiling and the rest of the room was decorated in black and white to match the pictures.

"I heard a lot about you Ms. Tiara."

"Oh really? What did you hear?"

"Don't worry, most of it was good shit, I heard about your ex man though, that's fucked up, I'm sorry to hear about that.

I turned my head trying to avoid the topic.

"As pretty as you are, I'm surprised that no one has tried to come and mend your broken heart sooner." He licked his sexy lips and I tried to overlook it and finish the conversation because he looked too damn good.

"Well I'm selective about who I talk too, plus I haven't been looking for a relationship. I've been trying to focus on me."

"Well I hope I'll be able to focus on you too. You seem like you don't let anybody get close to you, you're going to be a tough one."

"If you say so."

"See that's what I'm saying, you're sassy but I'm feeling it. I hope we can get to know each other a little better."

About an hour later, Ke-Ke and Shawn came walking back into the mansion. Ke-Ke looked at me, "T, I'm ready when you are, just let me know a'ight."

"I'm ready now Ke-Ke." I stood up waiting for Tony to stand up as well so that he could walk me to the door. He waited for me to walk past him and then he stood up to follow me. We stood in front of his front door. "Well it was nice meeting you Tony, I got your number so I'll make sure that I keep in touch."

"Well make sure you use it ASAP, matter fact, here is a hundred dollars, go buy you a cell phone so that I can always contact you." He pulled out a stack of money from his Gucci jean pocket, the thickness of the stack was ridiculous. Looking at that money made me see why Ke-Ke was so wrapped up into being with a baller.

After meeting Tony, things picked up quickly. We spoke everyday, quickly became best friends and eventually ended up becoming a couple. We completed each other; we were both hood but knew how to turn it on and off. I was like his secretary, he would give me the money to pay for his mortgage and other bills and if I had to put someone in check, I did it with a hood/business demeanor. I would make his runs with him and of course I knew so many people that I got him new customers. He was deeply in the game and I was in it with him making sure that things were in order and our bond was unbreakable. He was selling coke and weed so he had to teach me the ropes of how to weigh it, bag it and the whole nine yards. I let my guard down and was in it for love instead of money, well maybe both.

Tony would take me to the most expensive restaurants in Boston and we would eat lobster, steak, and shrimp, shit that I only ate once a year if that. He laced me in Gucci, Dolce & Gabbana, Louis Vuitton and whatever else I wanted. I was living in the hood feeling like a million bucks and finally happy again.

Tony's attitude was cocky but it was sexy to me, he was very confident and whenever we were in stores together and I would pick up a bag that I wanted, he'd be on his cell phone talking to one of his client's snapping his fingers at the sales associate to wrap up whatever I wanted. They loved to see us coming in the stores because they knew that Tony was a big spender.

Tony and I often spoke about him giving the game up and using his money to open something legit. He either wanted to start a mortgage company or to open up a restaurant in the hood. One way or another, I was trying to make sure that he wasn't in this game forever. There were only three ways out of the drug game, giving it up, losing everything or going legit and I was making sure Tony's game was tight enough to eventually turn legit.

Being with Tony, I didn't have to work, he didn't want me to because he said that it would take away from our time together. Every time we were together he broke me off money to use at my leisure and I would spend the majority of it on Sharod. I was totally in love again and not only did Tony's charm and money take me to ecstasy but the sex was off the chain!

Derek was a drug dealer too but not on a major level like Tony was. Sex with Derek was amazing but we were still young and inexperienced, well at least I was. The first time Tony and I had sex, he made sure that he fulfilled years of pleasure that I missed after losing Derek.

It was a hot summer day and I was wearing a short Christian Dior skirt which was easy access for Tony. We were in his mansion watching TV in his living room lying on his white soft bear skin rug. We popped a bottle of Dom Perignon and were watching Ice Cube's movie, *Next Friday*. He slid his hand up my skirt and pushed my panties to the side with his fingers and started circling my kitty. It had been so long since I felt that tingling sensation from a man that I was about to cum on the spot. He flipped my skirt over my stomach and pulled my silk Victoria panties down my legs and dove head first downtown making sure he licked, sucked and slurped every drop of my juices like he was dying of thirst. I was moaning and yearning for more as I had orgasm after orgasm. His tongue was like medicine that cured my sickness, I squeezed my eyes tight as I put both of my hands behind his head moving it in circles until I had the biggest, longest orgasm and couldn't handle it anymore. As I was trying to move his head up, he was forcefully keeping a grip on my clit with his mouth, this man was more than a pro, and he was making sure that I wouldn't forget about his skills. He finally lifted his head up looking at me smiling, he knew that he pleased me and then some.

He stood up, took off his jeans and boxers all at one time, revealing his nine inches of thickness that I was about to endure. As he got on his knees I pulled off my shirt and bra, he massaged my nipples with his tongue as I sat back enjoying him making my body his playground. He spread my legs and I prepared myself for penetration. He stuck his huge penis into my damn-near virgin kitty and stroked and stroked as I moaned for more. I scratched his back digging my nails deep into his skin as I got used to the motion and then I began winding my hips on him like a reggae dance.

"You like daddy's big dick," Tony asked. "Tell me you love daddy's big dick."

"I love daddy's big dick," I said.

Tony and I never used protection right from the beginning. I knew that I was being stupid but I enjoyed it raw just as much as he did. But with that came consequences.

Trè was getting out of jail in a couple days and I was excited for him to meet Tony. Sharod and my mom already met and adored him and I was hoping that things would be cool with Trè as well. I lied to my mom and told both her and Sharod that Tony worked for a prestigious law firm downtown Boston. Most likely she knew that I was lying but I just wanted to keep Sharod from admiring the drug dealer lifestyle.

I stayed the night at Tony's house the day before Trè came home. We got up early the next day to go to my house so that Trè and Tony could finally meet. My mom called my cell phone on our way there and told me that Trè was already home and that they were just waiting for us. Tony was about to take a left and pull up to my building but when he saw Trè on the outside of the building smoking a cigarette, he looked at Trè and said, "Aw shit!" He turned off his left blinker and kept driving straight.

I looked at him with a strange look on my face. "Where are you going Baby, you passed my crib?"

Tony looked like he was pissed off. "I had to, I just saw this nigga that robbed one of my boys."

My heart stopped. "That nigga is my brother Trè."

Chapter 12 – *Dilemma*

I knew things had to be too good to be true with Tony. Of all the drug dealers in Boston, Trè had to rob someone from Tony's block. Things in my life were finally somewhat smooth but drama always found its way back to me. I was hoping that Trè and his crew hadn't done anything too crazy like leave Tony's friend with one arm or something, Trè's crew was known for doing crazy shit like that. I was too nervous to elaborate with Tony on this subject but I knew that I had to.

I gathered up some courage and asked, "Which one of your people did he rob?" I was nervous awaiting his response.

"He robbed my man Mike, my homeboy you met last week. They were doing business together for a minute, and then your brother got on some grimy shit and set him up. He called him and told him to meet him on his block so that he could re-up. As soon as Mike pulled up, your brother got in the passenger seat and pulled out the toast on him. He ran him for all his shit; I mean this nigga took his jewelry *and* his weed. And he had the nerve to say some sarcastic shit like it was a pleasure doing business with you."

I almost laughed. I just knew that Trè's crazy ass would say something like that after robbing someone who he had done business with.

Tony pulled the car over and put it in park. "On some real shit Tiara, if you weren't with me and I saw that nigga by myself, I would have started airing the hammer out at him. I keep the toast under my seat, you already know."

I became fired up, this was my brother he was talking about. "Well since you already know that's my brother that shit ain't happening."

"Calm down T, Mike shouldn't have been meeting niggas on their blocks anyway. He know not to do business with stick-up kids, that ain't the first time that faggot ass nigga got robbed. But that's my man and you know how it is, his beef is mine."

"Damn! Mike seemed like he was cool as shit too, he don't even come around too much though, all this time we been together, I only seen the nigga a few times."

"Yeah that's because that nigga ain't a street cat, he's a hustler, not a banger."

I rolled my eyes. "Well fuck him then, shit. This is my family, we're gonna have to do something. You didn't put a name to the face when I told you my brother's name was Trè?"

"T, I never knew the niggas name, I just knew what he looked like. Mike's dumb ass didn't even know his name. I think he said they call him Little Man or something like that."

Tony put the car back in drive and we continued to talk on our way back to the building.

"I don't know about this shit T, for real. I know your brother's a real ass nigga, mad niggas heard of the dirt that he does but I really don't know what to tell you about this situation right now."

I shook my head, this couldn't be happening, I had to find some type of way for this not to turn out ugly.

I turned and looked at Tony as we pulled back in front of the building. "I'm gonna talk to Trè, my man and my brother can't be banging with each other, that shit just ain't happening. I know my family is going to be asking about you today Tony, I'll make some shit up but by the end of the night I'll let you know what's good."

We kissed each other good bye and I got out slamming Tony's car door and watched him as he pulled off. I stood in the same spot for a few seconds preparing myself to go inside.

Trè had already finished his cigarette and went back into the crib. I walked down the hallway up to my apartment door not knowing how I would talk to Trè about Tony. I slowly turned the key into the lock before turning the knob to open the door to greet Trè. As soon as I walked in, Trè was on the couch facing the door.

"Look at my baby sis all dipped up," Trè said smiling.

"Thanks bro, welcome home." I walked over to hug him, he stood to his feet and hugged me teasing. "You're still my little sis, I'll hem your little ass up."

My mom chimed in. "All the fighting your sister been out there doing, she'll give you a run for your money."

Trè let go of me putting up his two hands like he wanted to box.

"Oh please Trè, I'm sure you fought enough in jail." I said.

He put his hands down. "Don't even mention that shit hole."

"Who picked you up from jail anyway?" I asked.

"Bitch ass Javon picked me up."

"Oh word." I looked over at Sharod but still talking to Trè. "Sharod got big huh, look at him over there acting all shy, he's almost 14 and almost taller than both of us."

Sharod blushed while standing next to my mom in the kitchen then asked, "Tiara, where's Tony?"

I turned my head and tried to avoid his question. "He's mad cool Trè, he reminds me of you."

Trè put his two fists up like he was boxing again but this time aiming it towards Sharod teasing. "Can't no nigga be me Sharod, remember that."

Sharod put up his two fists and he and Trè began play fighting. I was glad that I was able to avoid talking about Tony. I went into the kitchen and saw a ton of aluminum pans full of food.

"Ma, what did you cook?"

My mom beamed proudly. "I made collard greens, yams, macaroni and cheese, turkey and gravy." The aroma of the soul food filled my nose and my stomach began to growl. My mom was actually sober today and she put her two hands on her hips and looked at me curiously. "I thought you said your friend was coming over to meet Trè?"

"Oh, he can't make it. Do you need help with anything?" I was hoping Trè didn't hear my mom question me while he was play fighting with Sharod but he did and he chimed in.

"What you embarrassed about the nigga T? What you got an old fat ugly ass muthafucka?"

My mom pointed her finger at Trè.."A'ight Trè, enough of all that cussing in my house, you sound like your father."

"My fault Ma." He looked back at me. "What up with ole' boy, I wanna meet the nigga, I didn't think I would like no nigga dealing with my sister but Derek was a cool ass nigga. What's this new niggas name again?"

"His name is Tony."

I watched as Trè let Tony's name roll around in his head."Tony, Tony where is he from?"

"Listen, we'll talk about him later, let's just chill and eat right now, I know you want some real food after eating all that nasty jail food."

Trè put his hand on his belly and started rubbing it in a circular motion.

"You ain't lying, I'm about to tear this food up, that jail food had my stomach twisted, I stayed on the toilet."

We all laughed at Trè as we sat down at the dinner table, made our plates and enjoyed a normal meal with the entire family for a change.

Usually when Trè got out of jail, he would go to his block and get updated on everything that's been happening since he'd been gone. This time, he stayed home the whole night chilling with the family. It was the perfect time for me to approach Trè about Tony. After dinner, he was in his room bobbing his head to some old beats that he had in his room reciting one of his hundred rhymes that he had written while locked up. He had one hand holding his notebook and the other hand was being waved and pointed in front of him as if he was on stage. His rhymes had always relaxed him so I knew that I had caught him in a mellow mood.

I slowly walked into his room, dragging my feet, I didn't want to do this but I knew that I had to. I was hoping that Trè would embrace the situation and help me come up with a solution. I didn't want any violence to arise from this, after all, they had beef and it would only take me to tell Trè where Tony and his people's were and it would be an all out war.

When Trè saw me come into his room, he turned down his music, sat on his bed looking at me with an expression on his face like what do you want. I sat down on the bed next to him.

"Trè, I have to talk to you about something."

He turned to face me, at this point the butterflies were doing more than flying in my stomach, they were in there making babies. My heart pounded and I had to gather as much courage as I could muster to tell my brother that I was fuckin' with one of his enemies.

"A'ight Trè, I ain't gonna bullshit you and tip toe around it." I inhaled deeply and released it. "My boyfriend Tony that I was telling you about told me that you robbed one of his boys."

Trè put one hand on his belly and started laughing. "So you're messing with a buster!"

I was still in serious mode and didn't think that what I said was funny. I was serious.

"Nah for real Trè, you robbed his boy Mike, y'all used to do business together until you ran him for all his shit."

He jumped up off the bed as if what I just said sparked his memory. "Hold up T, you're messing with Tony, T-Money?"

I looked up at him and nodded my head.

"Yeah I robbed that faggot ass nigga Mike, matter fact, niggas from the block was gonna get at T-Money too, them niggas always try to come around flossing and shit like they be asking to be robbed."

"Well we been together for a minute now Trè, Tony know you're my brother so I don't want no bullshit, I know how you are. I didn't want to bring him to the crib and there be some rah-rah shit between y'all."

Trè pursed his lips together. "T, you already know what it is with me and my niggas. Tony and his niggas know what up too. I robbed Mike and them niggas didn't do shit." He sat back on the bed so that he made sure his words stuck with me. "Let's keep it real, most of them niggas don't bang, they only hustle. I ain't thinking about them, they know the deal, you could bring the nigga through, bring him on over."

I looked at Trè shaking my head side to side. "Nah Trè, don't try to be funny, I ain't bringing him through for you to do some grimy shit to him, he's cool as shit and plus he don't really fuck with Mike like that anyway."

Trè relaxed his face and looked at me like he didn't care. "T, I don't care if he did fuck with Mike, I dare them niggas to think about doing something." Trè got on his knees and reached under the bed. He pulled out this big ass machine looking gun that you only see in the movies. He lifted it up and said, "You think I'm worried about anybody T?"

I looked that gun up and down examining every inch of it. It looked like it could take out an army. It was just like Trè to have a gun under the bed the whole time he was doing a bid. He didn't think about the fact that Sharod could've found it but, Trè's crazy ass never thought about stuff like that. He was too heavily wrapped into the streets to care about what was happening at home, I guess he was just trying to survive.

After Trè and I had our conversation, I felt somewhat comfortable about inviting Tony over. I knew that I couldn't trust Trè's word but I had no choice but to chance it. I told Tony that I had spoken to Trè about the situation and that he said that it would be no problem if I brought him to the crib. Tony knew Trè's rep on the street so he was reluctant at first but he wore balls of steal and eventually agreed to come over.

I didn't want to delay it any further, I wanted this situation out of the way ASAP. The next day, I brought Tony over to meet Trè. I felt like I was bringing him to meet an overprotective father or something. Tony came into my apartment with his cockiness written all over his face, he kept his head high and approached Trè who was on the couch watching TV with one leg stretched out on the couch and the other on the floor. He looked up at Tony, Tony extended his hand to give him dap. "What up, I'm Tony."

Trè looked at his hand, I thought that I was about to faint, I knew that if Trè left him hanging then Tony would probably get hostile for being made a fool of and if that would happen, then Trè would take it to levels unknown. After about two seconds, Trè put his other foot on the floor sat up and accepted Tony's dap.

Trè stood up and nodded his head toward the door, "Dog, can I talk to you out in the hallway for a second?" Tony agreed and Trè opened our apartment door leading Tony into the hallway.

My heart was galloping like a race horse at this point, I didn't know what was about to go down in that hallway so I stood inside my apartment with my ear to our hollow door listening, I heard Trè talking first, I couldn't believe how levelheaded he sounded.

"On the strength of my sister, we can squash this shit, I ain't putting no money in your pocket and you ain't putting none in mine."

"I respect that, the shit that happened with my man Mike, we'll just charge it to the game." I heard their hands smack and I quickly ran away from the door as they were coming back inside.

I couldn't believe that I was the cause of squashing one of Trè's beefs. Tony's boys were one less group of enemies on his hands but I didn't trust either one of them because you never know what they'll do once they are on the streets. For the time being, things were fine. Tony and I were back to our normal routine, taking me out to fancy restaurants and showering me with gifts. He made me feel like more than I thought I was worth. He always told me that I was beautiful and that I was his sunshine and that without sunshine, the world would be nothing.

I came into this relationship with the intentions of being a gold-digger and ended up surrendering my heart to the man of my dreams.

Tony was everything that every girl wanted: attractive, ambitious, wealthy, and not stingy and knew how to work his nine inches like a porn star. Most of all, he took a chick from the hood like me and wifed me like I was a Princess.

Tony and I had just finished having a night full of passionate yet wild sex and he dropped me off at home, my body was worn out and ready to meet my pillow. I headed straight for my bedroom, I was so drained. I was so worn out that I didn't even get in the shower.

My clothes still smelled like sex and my core was still moist from cumming so many times. But the bed was the only destination that I was heading for. I laid across my bed fully clothed, I snuggled up on top of my blanket as if it was a relaxing bath and as soon as I was about to close my eyes, I looked up and saw Sharod's shadow. His face showed an expression that I'd never forget.

"Tiara, one of Trè's boys just called Ma from the hospital, Trè got shot!"

I shot up like a bat outta hell. I ran in my
mom's room to check on her but she wasn't in
there. I yelled out to Sharod, "Where's Ma?"

"She's in the hallway," he said. I ran out in
the hallway of my building and saw my mom
asking one of our neighbors for a ride to the
hospital. Sharod was shook, he looked so nervous,
his eyes were full of concern. Trè was his idol and
the thought of him being dead was like a nightmare
come true, for all of us.

I tried to be the strong one and try to calm
them down and assure them that everything would
be okay. The truth was, I didn't know if things
would be okay. Taking that ride to the hospital
brought back memories of riding to the hospital to
see Derek. There was no way this could be
happening again. My body couldn't handle another
episode of seeing someone that I loved, lifeless on a
hospital stretcher. I closed my eyes and I tried to
hide my emotions as I said a silent prayer asking
God to please deliver my brother. A tear happened
to sneak out of one of my eyes but I wiped it before

Sharod or my mom could see it, I had to remain strong.

We finally arrived at the hospital, my mom and Sharod went to see what room Trè was in, but I needed a moment before I went to see Trè's outcome. As I paced the hospital lobby, my mom yelled out to me nervously, "Tiara, he's in room 803."

She and Sharod were taken to Trè's room by one of the nurses while I was still pacing the lobby. I put both of my hands on my head and grabbed my hair, what kind of hand did life deal to me, if Trè was gone, then whoever took him might as well take me too. I pulled out my cell phone to call Tony, it had just dawned on me that he was probably involved. He could have probably pretended to squash the beef with Trè but secretly still had a vendetta. He picked up the phone and I unloaded on him.

"Tony, Trè just got shot, I hope you didn't have anything to do with this shit. Tell me that you didn't try to distract me by fuckin' me while your boys made their move?"

Tony sounded confused. "What are you talking about T, is he a'ight?"

"Don't worry about him Tony, worry about your boys if they were involved because I swear on my life Tony, I'll get the burner and pop one of them niggas myself!" I began crying thinking about what I would see when I entered room 803. "Tony, for real, I know how niggas are when they say that they squash a beef, that shit never really dies."

"T, calm down, I promise you, I had nothing to do with that, I put that on everything. Matter fact, what hospital are you at? Do you need me right now? I don't like to hear you crying like that?" I could tell he truly had nothing to do with what happened to my brother.

"We're at Boston City hospital."

"A'ight, I'm on my way."

Chapter 13 – Decisions

I entered Trè's with my heart beating through my shirt. I was expecting no less than the worse. After dealing with bullshit after bullshit, I knew that the results would be more than just bad. I walked in the room slowly, my head was spinning and aching and I was feeling faint, I knew for sure that I was about to collapse and fall head first to the floor. I was expecting to hear my mom's loud cry or to see Sharod going hysterical pacing the room. Instead I entered the room with my mom and Sharod at Trè's bedside talking to him.

I raised my head to the ceiling and blurted out, "God is good!"

Trè's back, knee and calf on the same leg had been patched up. He had survived three bullets of a 9-mm. I rushed over to hug and kiss him like I haven't seen him in thirty years, I was cheesing from ear to ear. I was so thankful and happy that he was alive I wanted to kiss his feet. The thought of losing Trè was like me losing myself, he was my soldier, my big bro, my best friend and I needed him in my life. Trè looked up at me telling me to calm down.

I shot him a look. "Calm down? I ain't the one that got shot and this almost killed me."

"I ain't going no where T, niggas is hard to kill on my block," he said quoting Tupac.

I pushed his good leg over and sat on the hospital bed. "This ain't a rap, this is serious, real life stuff, don't scare us like that again."

Sharod shook his head looking at Trè, his eyes filled with ease that Trè was okay. "I was shook, I thought somebody bodied you," Sharod said.

Trè looked at Sharod with a shocked face. "Come here Sharod."

Sharod walked over and switched places with my mom.

"I ain't going no where you hear me. Whatever you need or want let me know, you're my little soldier, you're a warrior just like me, I heard about the little rep you created on the streets, you really remind me of myself"

My mom interrupted, "He ain't like you. He's far from being like you Trè."

Trè strained to sit up. "What is that supposed to mean Ma?"

My mom tried to clean it up. "Nothing, y'all are just both opposite."

I know my mom didn't want to believe that Sharod was starting to become involved in the streets just like Trè had. We both wanted to continue to think of Sharod as a baby, the innocent one. Maybe she thought Trè and I both were the bad seeds but she never actually came out and said it, but I sensed it.

Trè was still mad about my mom's comment, he started to argue through his pain because as he spoke I kept seeing his face twist in discomfort whenever he felt pain in his leg or back.

"Ma, it ain't about who I am, it's the environment, we live in the hood. Sharod is out here too, it's all about survival. I can't teach him how to be a man, he has to learn that on his own and without a father, our only father figure *is* the hood. When you grow up in the hood as a black man, your parents don't raise you, the streets do. You're either a: hustler, thug, pretty boy, athlete or a punk. Niggas in sports or niggas that get signed to rap labels usually make it out. There ain't many black working niggas from the hood because we all want our money the fast way. Other than that, you have to survive the best way you know how or you can end up lost in the game. Me for one, I ain't losing, I'm surviving and I'm going to show everything I know to Sharod so that he survives through this shit as well."

I interrupted, "Well one way or another, I'm getting Sharod out of here, out of this hood."

Sharod sucked his teeth. "Man, why y'all always talking about getting me outta here, I'm straight, stop talking about this."

The nurse walked into the room "There's someone named Tony in the lobby, I told him that there are only three visitors allowed."

I jumped off Trè's bedside. "Okay, tell him that Tiara will be coming out in a second."

The nurse agreed and left the room. I walked by my mom and Sharod to bend over to talk to Trè. "Tony didn't have nothing to do with you getting shot right?"

Trè whispered back, "Nah, I was popping at the same niggas that killed Taqwon, we been beefing with them niggas for years but remember that big ass gun I showed you from under my bed?"

"Yeah," I said.

"That shit jammed, that's how the niggas were able to hit me up like this."

I was relieved, thank God Tony had nothing to do with this, but I felt bad that I came off to Tony like he was an enemy. I walked out into the lobby to meet Tony. He was pacing back and forth. He wore a mask of worry on his face that made me love him even more.

When he saw me, he rushed over to me, "T, baby, you a'ight, is Trè a'ight?"

He hugged me. "Yes, I'm okay and Trè's fine."

"I can't believe your crazy ass thought I had something to do with your brother getting shot." He said,

I gave him the puppy look. "I'm sorry Tony, I just met tragedy too many times, you never know who did what anymore, and I'm just tired of all this bullshit."

Tony looked at me, the hospital lights beamed on his teddy bear brown eyes; I could see the sincerity in his eyes when he asked. "T, I want you to move in with me, I want to take care of you." I looked at Tony, my mouth was open collecting air, and I didn't know what to say back to him, his question came out of no where.

I thought about my mom, she needed me to take the liquor bottles out of her hands when she got carried away. I thought about Sharod, who would be there to steer him in the right direction. Then I thought about Trè, he didn't trust anyone on the streets so he needed me to be the person that he confided in about all his dirt. My mouth was open so long a fly could have flown in it. Tony was looking at me waiting for my response.

"I don't know Tony, you have to give me some time."

Tony scrunched up his forehead. I could tell that I hurt his feelings. "Give you time to think about what? Why wouldn't you want to get out the hood?"

I interrupted him. "It's not that Tony, it's just that this isn't an easy decision."

"Tiara, you can't be the one to hold your family down all the time, you have to think about yourself. We are Tony and Tiara, TNT, together we could blow shit up, let me take you away from all this shit and give you what you deserve."

He grabbed me and held me tight and I melted in his arms as my eyes began to tear up. I wanted to just say yes and run away with him but I knew that my family needed me more than ever. Tony wanted a solid answer but I had to at least sleep on his proposition, thinking about my family was holding me back. Moving in with Tony meant that I would be out of the hood, eating right, living right and headache free. But at my mom's house, that meant total anarchy, no order at all, I was like the mediator for the entire household. I kept us together, I kept us on the right track and I needed my little brother to stay focused so I wanted to mold him.

I woke up early the next morning thinking about Tony's proposition. My thoughts were interrupted by a bunch of dudes talking in the next room. I knew that Trè was still at the hospital so it couldn't be his boys. I got out of the bed and walked down the hallway to listen to their conversation, it was coming from Sharod's room.

I walked up to his door and paused to listen to what they were talking about, something told me that I needed to hear this conversation.

"Sharod, I got the drop on them niggas that shot your brother, let's go bring it to them niggas."

My eyes lit up, my mouth dropped to the floor, I couldn't believe this was coming out of the mouth of one of Sharod's friends, then I heard Sharod say, "Hell yeah, I'm down, let's clean all them niggas up."

I was totally stunned at what I heard. I was so much in tune with Sharod being my little brother not knowing that he was out here in the streets just like Trè was. I spent too much time with Tony and too little time with Sharod, I was only giving him money like the money was raising him, I felt like I failed at what I tried to accomplish with him.

I rushed back to my room and called one of my girls to vent before I confronted Sharod. I grabbed the phone, sat on my bed and dialed her number I was patting my foot on the floor hoping that my homegirl picked up.

"Hello?"

"Karen, what you doing?"

"Nothing, sitting here watching my cousin's bad ass kids what's up with you?"

"Girl, tell me why Sharod got all these little niggas in my crib talking about riding out for Trè."

"Girl where you been? That's nothing new, these little niggas are out here banging harder than these older niggas."

"But this is my little brother Karen, my baby brother, little Sharod."

"Well your *baby brother* is sneaky. He's hiding his dirt from you T, I can't believe you didn't know he was out here banging. Sharod is not sweet little baby face Sharod anymore. I heard he be leading the little niggas that he be running with. Matter fact, this new nigga I'm talking to knows Sharod, mad niggas respect him off top because of Trè. The nigga I'm talking to is almost thirty years old, I was like what the fuck are you doing knowing Sharod, he was like that's his little man, he's a banger."

"Damn Karen, I feel old, you know I usually know what be going on out here, he kept this shit under wraps."

"You ain't getting old, you just be with Tony, ain't nothing wrong with it, you ain't missing nothing around here. Shit, I wish a nigga could take me away once and a while."

"Damn, this shit is crazy. I gotta go and check him about what I heard. I don't want him out here riding out for Trè. Plenty of niggas are gonna be doing that, I gotta get him away from around here." I shook my head and looked up to the ceiling. "A'ight girl, I gotta go, I'll hit you up later a'ight."

Karen tried to catch me before I hung up. "Yo T!?"

"What up?"

"Don't stress a'ight, Trè won't let nothing happen to Sharod, you know that. I just had to let you know because I know how much you love you some Sharod."

I chuckled. "Thanks Karen, I'll holla at you later."

I hung up with Karen and sat on my bed for a minute to gather my thoughts. I stood up and started walking towards Sharod's room. While walking down the hall, I peeked in my mom's room, her body was spread across her bed with an empty bottle of Mad Dog 20/20 on the side of her. I heard a noise like papers being shuffled around in her room. I pushed her door open to get a better look. I wasn't expecting to see what I saw. One of Sharod's friends was going through my mom's purse.

I looked at him like it was my purse he had in his hands. "Muthufucka get the fuck out of my mother's room!" I charged over to fight him ignoring the fact that he was a dude. I yelled out for Sharod, "Sharod, come here, hurry up!" He rushed into my mom's room with a few of his friends following behind him. "Sharod, your sneaky ass friend was in here going through Ma's purse." I socked him in the jaw with my fist as hard as I could. He looked at me stunned. I had my game face on. "What muthufucka, I dare you to hit me back!"

He held his jaw and tried to talk through his closed mouth, "Yo Sharod she's lying."

"Oh you're calling me a liar, then what the fuck are you doing in my mother's room nigga?"

I didn't need to do anything else, Sharod and his boys rushed him and hemmed him up to the wall. Then they grabbed him and took him out in the hallway of my building and stomped the shit out of him like they were playing kick ball with his body. All of Sharod's friends had ill grills on while stomping the dude with their Timberland boots. Everyone was mad at the fact that this nigga really came over disrespecting the crib of the leader of their crew.

"You disrespected my crib nigga? You done fucked up!"

Sharod backed everyone up, he reached his hand into his pants and pulled out his gun. He began pistol whipping the dude until he was unrecognizable. He was beating him in the face so bad with that gun that one of his boys had to grab him and try to take it out of his hand.

"Chill Sharod that nigga look dead!"

The nigga wasn't dead, but he was all fucked up, his face was covered in blood and he had stopped screaming after awhile because I guess he couldn't feel the pain anymore.

I stood looking at my baby brother, Sharod had a little bit of me in him and a whole lot of Trè.

I went back in the crib to wake my mom up. "Ma, wake up, wake up!" I shook her body.

She tried to push me away and roll over to stay asleep. "No Ma, you're waking up now! Do you know you was about to get robbed?"

I used force and I pulled my mom out of bed with my hands underneath her shoulders pulling her to her feet. I drug her over to the mirror standing her up. "Look at you Ma, you drink everyday, you don't even know what be going on in your house, you're always worried about someone being a good example for Sharod when you're not a good example for none of us."

I had to finally be brutally honest with my mom I was tired of this bullshit.

"Put me back in the bed Tiara!" Her words slurred and she positioned her body towards the bed. "I don't have time for this!" she said.

I grabbed her face and made her face the mirror. "Look at yourself, what happened to my mom, what happened to the strong independent Mom who used to go above and beyond to raise her kids?"

My mom burst out in tears, she started balling something serious. "I failed my kids Tiara, I have nothing to provide for y'all, just leave me alone, I'm an adult, and I don't have to answer to you."

"You're right Ma, I'm gonna leave you alone because you're an adult, matter fact, I'm moving out."

I let go of her and started heading towards the door to leave her room. I turned around. "Oh, and I'm taking Sharod with me."

I went into Sharod's room, he was in there changing his clothes taking off the bloody clothes that his friend had stained from being pistol whipped. "Sharod pack your bags, we're moving out of here."

He turned around looking at me confused, "Huh, I ain't leaving Ma."

"Don't worry about Ma, this is the only way she'll pull herself together, you can't stay here, this household is unstable."

"T, I can take care myself, y'all all need to stop worrying about me."

"Sharod, I'm not playing, pack your stuff up, I'm calling Tony to come get us."

"Where are we going?"

"To Tony's."

Sharod finally gave in and started packing his clothes. As I went into the room to call Tony, I heard my mom in Sharod's room begging him not to leave her. I grabbed my cell phone to call Tony.

"Hey Baby, what's up?"

I got right to the point. "Tony listen, I thought about what you asked me and I think I'm gonna move in with you."

I could tell Tony was smiling on the other end. "That's what's up baby, when are you gonna make it official?"

I hesitated to tell him that Sharod would be moving with me but I knew that I had to tell him because it was the only way that I would go. "I want to make it official as soon as possible but first I have to ask you something."

"What's up?"

"I want Sharod to move in with us." The phone was silent for a second. I anticipated his answer hoping that he wouldn't think of me as a burden with baggage.

"A'ight, that's my little nigga, of course he can come."

I closed my eyes in relief. "Thank you Tony, I love you so much. Do you think you can come get us now?"

"Now? Y'all packed and everything?"

"Yeah, there's drama over here, come quick okay."

"A'ight, I just have to go pick up some money from a few people and then I'll be right there."

"A'ight baby hurry."

I went into Sharod's room and my mom was wilding out.

"You ain't going nowhere Sharod!"

Sharod looked up at me. His eyes were full of sadness, he didn't want to leave our mom but he knew as well as I did that this would be the best for her. It was time for her to focus on herself and get her drinking together.

Ma was pulling all the clothes that Sharod had packed in his bag and put them back into his drawers.

"Tiara, could you get her please?" He rubbed my Ma's back and tried to talk to her calm so that she wouldn't be so dramatic. "Ma, just chill, it's only gonna be temporary okay?" He tried to assure her.

I gently grabbed her and tried to escort her out of Sharod's room. She stopped screaming and crying and let me lead her out.

"A'ight Sharod, I got her. Take your bags to the front and then come get mine. Ma will be a'ight."

My mom started screaming at the top of her lungs again. "Nooooo!!! Don't take my baby!" She turned around and ran back into Sharod's room. She started pulling on his shirt. He grabbed his bags and tried to head for the door. My mom was pulling on the back of his shirt stretching it out like a bridal gown's tail and was dragging on the ground holding it while Sharod headed for the door with his bags. "Don't leave me Sharod please!"

Sharod turned to look at me, "Tiara get Ma." He tried to break her hands loose of his shirt. "I love you Ma, stop bugging like this okay. I'm not a baby, I'm gonna be alright, it's only temporary."

After Sharod freed his shirt of my mom's grip, she laid on the floor crying like a baby. I knelt down to grab her and stand her up. "Ma, we ain't going far, we will still come over here I just want you to focus on you. You should be relieved that Sharod is going to be out of the hood and in a better neighborhood."

Ma finally calmed down a bit, or better yet she calmed herself down. When I stood her up, she headed for the kitchen and poured herself a tall glass of cheap Vodka from the fridge.

I left her soaking in the kitchen and I went into my room. I grabbed and threw all of my clothes into black trash bags and waited for Sharod to come back in to take them to the front of the building. I looked at my room, I knew I had slept my last night in my full size bed. I was leaving my childhood, teenage and little girl years behind me and was starting a new one living with my man. I felt empty inside, we lived in the building for so long and I felt like a kid parting from their favorite blanket. I reflected on the memories that I would leave behind and most of all, leaving my mom.

I turned around and turned my back on the half empty room and headed for my mom. She was sitting at the kitchen table drinking with a blank expression on her face staring out the window. Tears were rolling down her cheeks and she didn't say a word.

I bent to kiss her on her moist cheek, I whispered in her ear, "Mom, I love you." And I headed for the front door. I turned around one last time to take a look at the apartment that I was practically raised in and I smiled. I had come a long way. I said out loud, "Thank you Jesus!"

When I went to the front of the building where Sharod was sitting at with our bags waiting for Tony, I noticed a crowd of girls were beside him being nosy. Little girls always flocked around when they saw Sharod. Most of the girls were from the projects down the street and they just happened to see him outside. In other words they saw him from their windows and wanted to come and be fast. I opened the front door and one of the fast little girls who was sticking her boobs and ass out making her back arched looking like a damn camel asked, "Are you moving Sharod?"

I cut her completely off storming out of the door before Sharod could answer, "Mind your business!"

The group of girls looked at me wondering how I just came out of nowhere butting in their conversation. They gave me a look that let me know they wanted to pop off at the mouth but my grill was more dominating and the little chicks knew my rep and knew not to utter one out of order word my way. They turned to look back at Sharod and the little girl with the arch in her back said, "A'ight Sharod, we'll see you later kay? Hope you ain't going far." They turned around and headed up the street.

Sharod grew up to be a fine young man. If I was a young girl, I would have had a crush on him too. He had that silky golden brown complexion and soft silky jet black hair, I guess that was the half Puerto Rican part of him from Orlando's side, and the extremely cute face, long eyelashes and perfect cheek bones from my mom's side of course.

"T, you're mad rude, you know I wasn't gonna tell them where we are moving to."

"I ain't rude, them little hoe's need to mind their business, she had her back arched all in your face, if she was any closer to you, her nipple would have went in your mouth."

Sharod put his hand on his stomach and started cracking up. "T, you're crazy, I'm good on these chicks though, I want my money right first, I'm trying to ball out like you and Tony."

"Sharod please, we are far from balling, Tony has just been smart about where his money goes that's all. Oh and you better make sure not to let your little homeboys know where we are moving to either."

"Chill T, I ain't telling no one, I'm glad we are moving in the cut, too many people knew about us living here. I wish Trè could move with us too, but I don't want Ma here by herself."

Sharod used to be a Momma's boy growing up. Trè never took him anywhere so he clung to my mom. I knew he didn't want to leave her but she had to face this alcohol problem and hopefully quit.

Tony finally pulled up to the front of the building. I saw his smile even before the car pulled up. His wish had finally come true and I surrendered and was now moving in with my man. I hoped that this would be the right decision, for me and especially for Sharod.

Chapter 14 – Backstabbers

We pulled up to the garage at the top of the hill where Tony's house was and Sharod's eyes lit up. He looked at Tony, "Daaaamn, this is how you doing it T-money?"

Tony smiled. "This ain't nothing."

"Yeah right, this crib is HOT!!" Sharod's mouth dropped in amazement.

We got out of the car, Tony and Sharod headed for the trunk and took out our clothes. Tony handed me my new set of keys and we headed inside. Sharod walked in the door and dropped the bags and started looking around with his eyes bucked in amazement. He looked up at the spiral staircase and then glanced in the living room at the butter soft leather couches and expensive pictures, he looked down at the marble floors and put his hands up to his mouth. "Yo, this is dope, this crib is off the hook!"

Tony tilted his head towards the guest room. "Come on, let me show you your room."

Sharod followed Tony like he was still the little kid that I knew, his smile was large, and he was so excited to be in a luxurious house.

I smiled as they walked away, I was glad to see that my baby brother was happy and most of all safe. I walked up the stairs and went into the room that Tony and I would now share. I sat on his king size bed and fell straight back looking up at the ceiling. I felt free again, I felt like most of my worries were gone, I was out of the hood and had my little brother under my wing. I thought about my mom and how I hoped that she would change, I thought about what Trè would think when he came home from the hospital and realized that we were gone. Tears began to fall down the sides of my eyes. I heard Tony coming up the stairs so I quickly wiped my eyes but he had already noticed that I was crying.

He crawled on top of me and his tongue found its way to my neck.

"Relax Tiara, this is how I'm going to make you feel everyday." He unbuttoned my top and freed my breast from my bra. He began gently caressing my nipples with his tongue taking his time licking and sucking on them, he looked up and whispered, "I'm gonna take care of you from now on."

I couldn't say anything, Tony made me feel so safe, so secure, and he was my heart, my best friend, my crutch. He pulled down my pants and I closed my eyes surrendering my body to him freeing myself of stressful thoughts. I felt his tongue slurping and slithering and sucking on my kitty. I closed my eyes tighter and let out a loud moan. He took me to an ecstasy that I'd never reached before.

After I climaxed, we just lay holding each other, I was drained and just wanted to go to sleep in his arms. I wanted him to know that I appreciated him and that I would be lost without him. I gripped him tight as I lay on his bare chest. "Tony, I love you so much and I appreciate everything that you've done for me." He gripped me tighter and rubbed his hands through my hair. I closed my eyes relaxing my head on his chest. He shook my shoulder when he noticed that my eyes were closed.

"T, don't go to sleep yet, I have to show you something." Tony sat up and I sat up with him at the same time, once he stood to his feet, I laid back down in the bed, I wasn't finished coming off of my orgasm high.

"Baby, can it wait till later?"

"Nah T, come here, I got something for you."

I lazily sat up and walked over to Tony, he held my waist with one hand as we walked side by side down the stairs and he led me out to the garage.

"Okay Tony, why are you showing me your Lexus?"

"You mean *your* Lexus." He handed me the keys.

I took them in my hand. "You're joking right?"

"Nah, I was waiting for you to move in with me so that I could show you what I meant when I said that I'm gonna take care of you, you're my wifey."

I let out a blunt scream and jumped up and down. "Tony, you're really giving me your Lex coupe?"

"Yeah T, it's nothing, if I'm styling, my baby girl should be styling to."

I grabbed Tony and jumped up on him wrapping my legs around his waist. I started kissing him sticking my tongue down his throat like I was reaching for his lungs. I wanted him to know that I appreciated everything. When I let Tony go, I looked up and thanked God for allowing me to be so lucky.

"Okay baby, you know I have to go pick the girls up for a joy ride real quick."

"Slow down T, I got some lobster, steak and shrimp for you and Sharod inside."

Tony and Derek were the only two people that presented expensive food like that in my

257

presence. I didn't have to do a thing in the kitchen, Tony prepared everything and he, Sharod and I ate our food watching a Chris Tucker movie. We laughed and joked all night like we were a real family and it all felt so good. I looked over at my baby brother while he was talking to Tony, his long silky braids and his innocent smile was everything that I lived for, he was so handsome and grew up so fast. I was so proud of myself and during dinner I made it known that Sharod only had to go to the hood for school, other than that he should spend the majority of his time in the cut with us.

I cut dinner short leaving Sharod and Tony still eating, it was time to go joy riding.

I kissed both of my men on the cheek, "I'll be back later on tonight y'all." I grabbed my purse and headed for the garage smiling all the way to my new Lex.

I grabbed my cell phone and called all the girls one by one and then scooped them all up.

"Where y'all wanna go?" I said with one hand on the wheel cruising like I had the car for years. I had my sunroof open to let the wind blow through my hair and turned on the screens behind my headrest.

"Let's cruise up Blue Hill Ave and see who's out, we gotta roll by the clubs in these wheels stunting on these bitches, this car is fuckin hot!" Renée said from the backseat.

Ke-Ke was in the front seat, she had taken over being my side kick since Tamika was out of the picture and we ended up being closer than Thelma and Louise. We cruised down Blue hill Ave rolling by the clubs slowly so that everyone could get a good glimpse at the twenty-two's on my coupe.

"T, pull over right here, I think I see Shawn." Ke-Ke's loud mouth screamed out of the window, "Shawn! I know you ain't out here talking to none of these chickenheads."

The group of girls he was talking to looked over at my car rolling their eyes. Karen and Renée were in the backseat sucking their teeth and rolling their eyes at the fact that Shawn was out there trying to holla at the chicks. They immediately started talking about how much of a dog Shawn was.

Karen in particular kept rambling on about how he was a dog and how Ke-Ke needed to leave him alone. We just laughed and ignored her because she always had something bitchy to say.

Shawn walked up to the car and bent down to look inside. "What y'all doing out in Tony's whip?"

I stretched over to Ke-Ke's window. "You mean *my* whip."

"Oh word he gave you the wheels?" Shawn asked.

He stuck his head in the car and checked the backseat. "What up y'all?" He said to Karen and Renée.

Renée spoke but Karen ignored him looking out of her window on the opposite side of the car.

"Shawn you better not be out here talking to these hoes, you didn't even tell me you was going out to the club tonight."

"Damn, a nigga gotta tell you everywhere he goes now?"

Ke-Ke reached her hand out and tapped him on his torso. "Don't be fresh." She put on her serious I need money face. "Shawn, I'm going shopping tomorrow, you got any money on you for me?"

"Damn Ke-Ke, you always hitting a nigga up for dough." He put his hand in his pocket and pulled out three crisp one hundred dollar bills and handed them to Ke-Ke. "Here. I'll call you later. I'm going over Tony's after the club so make sure you go home with Tiara." He stuck his head in the window and gave Ke-Ke a peck on the lips and then I pulled off.

We rolled up all the windows, I turned up the radio and we were grooving to Ciara's song *"Oh."* We were all singing the words cruising slow on Blue Hill Ave.

"Around here we ride sloow, Oooh!!!" We were snapping our fingers, bobbing our heads

having a good time for a change. Ke-Ke turned
down the music and pointed at one of the clubs.

"Ain't that Takia and Monique? Pull up next
to them T."

I crept up on Takia and Monique slowly, my
dark tints and twenty-two's made it seem like we
were dudes pulling up to them to try to holla. They
were looking at the car like some gold diggers ready
to holla back. Takia fixed her hair and started
putting on some lip gloss. The looks on their faces
when we rolled down the window was as if they
saw a ghost. Ke-Ke took the half full juice bottle
that she got in my car with, opened the top and
threw juice all over their cheap ass outfits.

Renée and Karen screamed out from the
back seat, "Y'all fake-ass, broke, bitches!!!"
I peeled off leaving skid marks in the street, we
laughed all the way to a local pizza shop in Grove
Hall. We sat and talked about the latest gossip, how
proud they were of me taking Sharod out of the
hood and how they were happy for me and Tony.
For some reason whenever we brought up Shawn's

name Karen would roll her eyes and change the subject but we all ignored it thinking it was typical Karen.

Later that night I dropped everyone off except Ke-Ke and we headed back to Tony's around 1:30 in the morning. I was tired but relieved that I had a good night after all of the drama that I went through earlier at my mom's. When we were halfway to the door, I saw someone knocking. I had to squint my eyes for a better view and noticed that it was a female.

"T, who the fuck is that?" Ke-Ke asked.

"I don't know who that bitch is but I'm surely about to find out." I started speed walking up to the door. "Excuse me who are you looking for?"

The girl turned to look at me with an ill grill. "My man, who are you?"

I turned to look at Ke-Ke. "Oh hell no Ke-Ke, you hear this bitch?" I turned back in the girl's direction. "Your man huh, I know you don't mean Tony?"

"Yes Tony, and as I said, who are you and who the fuck are you calling a bitch?"

I looked at Ke-Ke. "Damn Ke, this bitch got me fucked up." I looked back at the girl. "Listen here baby girl, my name is—" I didn't even finish my sentence. I punched her in the face knocking her off her stilettos. Ke-Ke joined in and we were kicking her in the sides of her stomach while she was on the ground trying to block our kicks.

"Don't you ever question me bitch!" I yelled as we kicked her.

The girl was on the ground screaming, "Get off of me, get the fuck off of me!"

The door opened and Sharod and Tony came out. "T, what are you doing?" Tony pulled me into the house while I was trying to get in more kicks to her body. "Ke-Ke you get in here too!"

Sharod grabbed Ke-Ke's shoulders. "Come on Ke-Ke, that's enough."

When we were all in the house Sharod was looking at me and Ke-Ke who were still in drama mode. "Who was that, y'all fucked her up!"

"Sharod can you go in your room for a second, I need to talk to Tony."

Ke-Ke walked over to Sharod, "Come on, let them talk." She looked back at me while walking with Sharod. "T, make sure you check that nigga, that's some disrespectful shit."

"Ke-Ke, I got this, just go in there with Sharod for a second." I waited until I heard the door slam and I smacked the fuck out of Tony.

"I knew this shit was too good to be true! You're a fuckin dog, you ain't no different than any other nigga."

Tony held his cheek, I could tell it was stinging because I put a lot of hurt into that smack.

"T, you're trippin' right now, that ain't my bitch, that's a slut that I fucked back in the day, it was way before you, the bitch just can't let go."

"All niggas give excuses like that Tony. Fuck you! I'm getting my shit and I'm bouncing." I stormed up the stairs, I was pissed, my head was throbbing and anger had my stomach in knots. Tony followed behind me begging and pleading. "T, you can't leave me, I ain't fucking no other chick."

"So why the fuck was she here then Tony? The bitch had her hair done and that short ass skirt was screaming I wanna get fucked."

"Fuck all that, that bitch took it upon herself to come here, what I look like telling a bitch to come to my crib where me and my girl stay at?"

"I don't know Tony, but you should have thought about that before I saw her."

"T, you're my heart, you're down for a nigga, you don't have a long ass track record of fucking niggas, you're loyal and you're beautiful. That's hard to find, real talk. You ain't going anywhere."

Tony took my clothes out of my hands and tried to sit me on the bed.

"Tony move, it's over! Move!" I tried to shove him out the way so that I could continue to put my clothes back in my bags that were still mostly packed.

Tony came out the cut. "Marry me T."

"Tony I don't have time for this."

"Nah I'm serious, I was going to ask you anyway. Marry me, I wanna show you that you're my only girl and that you can trust me."

"Tony, I don't have time for head games. The last man I was with fucked my best friend and now I found a bitch at the front door of my new man's house. I don't trust NO NIGGA."

"Baby, you can trust me, don't do this."

I couldn't believe I had broken Tony down. The hardcore hustler I was used to dealing with was actually begging me to stay. I didn't know whether to believe him or trust my women's intuition. I just couldn't believe that this bitch was here to see and possibly fuck my man.

I heard Ke-Ke's loud mouth yelling from downstairs. I managed to get by Tony so that I could see what was going on from the top of the stairway.

I looked over and saw that Ke-Ke was arguing with Shawn. She had his phone in her hand and he kept reaching for it but she was moving it behind her screaming about some chick's number that she saw in his phone a bit too much. "So this is who you been fucking?"

Shawn finally got his phone from Ke-Ke's hand and grabbed her by her hair pulling her towards the front door.

Tony yelled down the stairs, "You a'ight dog?"

"Yeah, I'm going to take this bitch home, I'll holla at you later."

"Bitch!" I yelled. "Shawn don't be disrespecting my girl!"

He slammed the door and ignored me.

"Tony, I don't know what's up with your boy but you better check that nigga."

"Fuck all that, I ain't done talking to you. You didn't give me an answer yet."

"You want an answer Tony? I'll give you one. Every man in my life has fucked up or fucked me over. From my father who didn't give a shit about me, to Trè who was just as lost as I was. Then there was Derek, he loved me hard and then made me fall hard. He fucked my best friend and then he lost his life just when I wanted to tell him that I forgave him. I mean, even the first boy that I kissed was killed. The only man in my life that hasn't failed me is Sharod. I'm going to try damn hard to make sure that he ends up on top." I pointed in Tony's face. "Now, let me talk about your ass. I move in with you wearing my heart on my sleeve once again and you have one of your bitches coming by to see you? I don't have good luck with men in my life so we might as well end it now."

"For the last fuckin' time, I didn't tell that bitch to come over here and I'm not going to say that shit again!" Tony started becoming defensive and it seemed like he was giving up on convincing me.

"You know what Tony, I just need to get some air, just give me my space right now."

Tony put his hands up. "I respect that."

He let me walk out of the room in peace and I headed downstairs to check on Sharod. I knocked on Sharod's door and then walked in. He was sitting on his bed and stood up when I walked in. "You straight T? Who was that chick y'all was fuckin' up?"

"That was no one, don't even worry about it."

"You sure? Did you hear Ke-Ke and that dude arguing? As soon as he came, she grabbed his phone. After that, shit got real dramatic."

"Well don't worry about that either Sharod, you'll see when you get in a relationship, shit can get hectic sometimes."

"I'm good on relationships, I ain't wifing no chick, I'm keeping it just like I have it now, drama-free. When I'm old enough to want to settle down, I'll have my girl pop out like two seeds, but right now, I'm good on the drama."

"What! My baby brother is talking about having kids? That's what's up, you know I'm gonna spoil them rotten."

Sharod sat back on the bed and switched his mood to serious. "T, I been thinking about Ma, you think she's a'ight? You think she'll really get herself together?"

I sat on the bed next to him as my eyes filled with tears. His concern was so genuine and it hurt like hell to see him like that. "Yeah Sharod, Ma's gonna be straight."

"She's killing herself T, drinking all day everyday, she don't listen to no one who be trying to tell her to chill on the drinking."

"Sharod, I have always been there for you so trust me and take my word for it, I promise Ma will be fine."

"A'ight, I just feel bad that she's home by herself."

"Don't feel bad, this is what she needs." I reached over and hugged Sharod.

"I'm going to go out and get some air, I'm gonna stop by Ke-Ke's and check up on her and I should be back in like a half a'ight?"

"A'ight I'm gonna be chilling in here watching my new big screen ya know."

I laughed. "My baby brother always knows how to cheer me up, I'm glad you like your room and your new big screen."

"Hell yeah I like it," he laughed.

"A'ight, I'm out, I'll see you when I get back." I started walking towards Sharod's door to exit, he said, "Love ya big sis, thanks for looking out for me."

"No need to thank me, you're apart of me, what's mine is yours." I walked back over to kiss him on the cheek, "A'ight baby bro, you're still my little boo boo and always will be." I joked.

"Yeah a'ight, see you when you get back."

"A'ight, love you."

"Love you too."

I got in my car and headed towards Ke-Ke's crib. I had to check on my girl and plus I needed some time to get my head together regarding this Tony bullshit. I kind of believed him but I didn't want to sell myself short just in case he really called this bitch to come over because he thought I would stay out later or something. My mind was all twisted and I couldn't wait to hear Ke-Ke's opinion. Someone of Tony's caliber who was fine as shit with a lot of money would always have groupies flocking around in the midst. But you never know with niggas like him. I moved all of my shit to his crib and I would look like an asshole moving it back out after all the drama that happened at my moms. I hoped that by talking to Ke-Ke, some type of conclusion could be drawn out of all of this.

I pulled up to the side of the projects and called Ke-Ke on my cell phone and told her to come outside. The way that her voice sounded on the phone gave me an impression that she was still mad about her situation with Shawn because I could sense the attitude in her tone.

She got into the passenger seat of my car, slammed the door like she was crazy, sat down and folded her arms.

"Ke-Ke, you a'ight, what's going on with you and Shawn?"

"No I ain't alright and you know damn well why!"

"Hold the fuck up bitch, slow your roll. I don't even know what the fuck you're talking about."

"Well I find that hard to believe." She unfolded her arms and turned to look at me. "So you're telling me that you didn't know that Shawn was fucking Karen?"

My eyes lit up. "Hell no I didn't know that shit!"

"Well the bitch's number is all in his phone, I looked in the call log and he was talking to her like every day. I called her and the bitch had the nerve to tell me yes she did fuck him and she didn't think I would mind."

"So why the fuck would you think I would have known that, answer that Ke-Ke?"

"Come on T, me and Shawn are always around you and Tony, he had to have brought her around y'all."

"You have known me for years Ke-Ke, out of everyone, I remained one of the realest. I come here to check on your funky ass and you're coming out your mouth like I'm some grimy bitch you don't even know?" I turned to look out my window and shook my head. "You know what Ke-Ke, get the fuck out of my car, and while you're at it, cross me off your list bitch, I'm done with you."

"Fuck you too T, you walking around here with Tony like y'all on top of the world and if it wasn't for me, you wouldn't have even met him."

She opened the door to get out of the car. "Oh so the jealousy comes out of a bitch when she's mad huh? Good looking out on the hook-up bitch and we *are* on top of the world, sorry I couldn't say the same for you and Shawn. I'm off this!"

I sped off and didn't look back. I couldn't believe that bitch had the nerve to come at me backwards with some stupid shit. It hurt to have one of my closest girls accuse me of backstabbing her but I was on some grown woman shit, fuck it, I didn't need a friend like that.

I grabbed my cell phone to call Karen and she answered the phone expecting to hear my mouth. She knew how close Ke-Ke and I were and she figured that I was the first one that Ke-Ke told about her messing with Shawn.

She answered the phone with a nonchalant tone, "Yeah T, I know, you're calling to tell me I'm dirty right?"

"You damn right, what are you doing pulling some Tamika shit on Ke-Ke like a damn ho?

"Shit, Ke-Ke is always poppin' off at the mouth like she don't love a nigga and that she's only using niggas for money so shit, I wanted a piece of the pie too. Everybody ain't like you T, niggas don't like wifing chicks who been with mad niggas so I get it how I can."

"Fuck that stupid talk, don't try to use that as an excuse, niggas would respect you if you wasn't out here fucking with mad niggas, especially other niggas that are already taken."

"Well fuck it; what's done is done, but that bitch Ke-Ke better not be on some rah-rah shit when I see her."

"I ain't gonna let y'all fight, especially over some dog ass nigga."

"You know what, I don't even have to fight Ke-Ke because Shawn already burnt us both so I guess we both got what was coming."

"Yeah he's a dog and he was playing with both of y'all's head."

"Nah T, I'm talking about he burnt us literally, he gave me crabs."

"Oh hell no, that nasty muthafucka!"

Chapter 15 - Tragedy

I hung up the phone with Karen to call Renée, I had to talk to someone halfway sane. I filled her in on the situation between Ke-Ke and Karen.

"See y'all thought I was the chickenhead of the crew, Karen's bitchy ass was undercover."

"The whole situation is a mess, Shawn was double dipping within the crew. I can't believe Ke-Ke had the nerve to question me like I knew all about it. She pissed me off with that shit and I'm cutting her off. Shit, she knew about Tamika and Derek, she seen the shit with her own eyes, just because she was the one who told me about them two didn't mean that she told me as soon as it happened, she knew about it the whole time and decided to tell me when she was ready.

"I never called her out on it, I just charged it to the game. And Derek was my man, Shawn is just one of the niggas she's fuckin and just happed to catch feelings for.

"This is why I'm good on all this petty shit, as soon as shit is right and me and Sharod and Tony are settled, I'm going back to school and we are moving the fuck up out of Boston and away from all of this wackness, I don't need any phony friends around me."

"You're right about that. Damn T, what happened to us? We were all down for each other, it seems like the only one striving for a better life is you."

"We all need to be striving for a better life, who wants to keep living this hood shit? It ain't fun no more, we are grown woman and need to start acting like it."

I noticed that someone was clicking in on my other line. I took the phone away from my ear to see who was calling.

"Renée, I'm gonna hit you back, this is my mom clickin' in."

I clicked over. "What's going on Ma?"

My mom could hardly speak, she was crying so hard that she couldn't even utter out her words. "T-Tiara it's your brother!"

"Ma, calm down, what do you mean it's my brother? Trè ain't getting released from the hospital till tomorrow."

She finally composed herself enough so that I could understand her. "It's not Trè, it's Sharod, he's been shot! My baby has been shot!"

"Ma, what are you talking about, he's at the crib with Tony."

"Just hurry up and get here, hurry!!" She hung up and I quickly called Tony as I was speeding through the streets hoping that he would tell me that Sharod was safely in his room where I left him.

"Baby, please tell me that Sharod is there."

"Naw, I was about to call you, some older niggas came to get him. I saw him get in the car and

280

they pulled off by the time I got outside to see
where he was going."

"So you didn't ask him anything? He didn't
tell you where he was going, he just left?"

"Nah, that's what I was coming outside to
ask because when I peeped them through the
window, I saw that they all had on black hoodies.
There were mad niggas in the car, it looked like
they were about to go do a mission."

I got weak to my knees and swallowed a
gulp of despair. "Tony, I'm gonna have to call you
back." I was racing through the streets like I was
training for the Indy 500.

I was thinking about what Sharod's friends
were saying to him about finding the niggas that
shot Trè. I was so wrapped up in my own drama
that I forgot to confront Sharod about what I had
heard him and his friends talking about. As fast as I
was going it still seemed like it wasn't fast enough
and it took forever for me to get to my mom's.

When I finally pulled up to the building, my mom was already in the front waiting. She got in the car crying hysterically.

"Ma, calm down, we don't even know the outcome yet. Calm down," I said rubbing her back. I tried to compose myself for my mom's sake, but my insides were screaming like I was being tortured. I wanted to cry with her. How could someone shoot my baby brother? My precious baby brother. I wanted to scream, cry, hit someone or even kill someone. I wanted to talk to my little brother and hear him tell me that he was okay. My mom's screams got louder and she was screaming out, "My baby, they shot my baby." I turned up the music to drown her out.

We pulled up to the hospital and I didn't give a fuck if I was parked correctly or not. My mom and I ran out of the car and went straight to the receptionist desk in the emergency room. The same receptionist was at the desk that we had just seen when we were at the hospital for Trè.

I looked further down the hall at another entrance and I spotted a familiar patched up male with crutches. He was smoking a cigarette with tears in his eyes. It was my brother Trè, the last time I saw him cry was when his friend Taqwon got killed.

I tapped my mom who was about to see what room number Sharod was in. "Ma, I see Trè over there, come on."

We made it halfway to Trè when my mom decided that she couldn't walk any further. She put one hand on the side of the wall and bent over crying all the way down to her knees.

"Aaaaah, my baby, I want to see my baby!" She lifted her head up again screaming through her tears. "Treeee, please tell me my baby is okay, Trè please, tell me now!"

Trè put out his cigarette and headed towards us. He looked me in my eyes while he held my mom and he spoke through the hurt and anger with a single tear falling down his cheek and muffled out the words I never thought I would hear, "He's gone."

I looked at Trè not knowing how to react, he had to be lying. I had just left Sharod at Tony's and I told him that I would be right back. He couldn't be gone, he wasn't gone.

I just knew this wasn't happening. I took him out of the hood, he was safe, he didn't have to go to the hood for nothing but school.

That's when I became angry. Why did Sharod leave the house, what was he thinking? I needed answers, I needed to see him. I still didn't believe this was true. My mom past out in Trè's arms, he tried to hold her up and balance on his crutches. I could tell it was painful for him because his wounds were still fresh. I tried to help him but we had to call for a nurse.

"Yo nurse, we need help!" Trè signaled a nurse passing by. "Can you help my mom she just fainted?"

The nurse rushed over by the receptionist desk and got a wheel chair for my mom. When the nurse wheeled my mom away, Trè and I stood looking at each other. I felt like we were six and eight again, I felt lost, I felt cold.

"We're all we got now sis." He shook his head."They took our little brother away."

Trè composed himself and had a look of revenge all over his face. "I'm leaving this hospital right now to hit the streets, niggas are on there way to get me right now. I'm killing whole fucking families, I don't give a fuck. Niggas fucked up Tiara, they fucked up bad."

I didn't know what to do or say, part of me wanted to tell him to calm down and think rational so that we wouldn't lose him too. The other part of me wanted to ride out with him and kill whoever was involved for taking Sharod. I was completely confused.

I thought about what Derek's mom had told me when he passed away, she told me that unless I saw him, I wouldn't get closure. I muscled up some courage, I had to say good-bye to my baby brother,

I had to see him because I was still in disbelief, "Trè, take me to his room, I have to see him."

Trè shook his head. "Sis on some real shit, I can't go back in there, when niggas called up here and told me that he was here, I didn't believe them. When the nurse took me into the room to see him, that shit blew my fuckin mind."

"Trè, just tell me the room number, I gotta see him, this shit still don't seem real to me."

"He's in room 701, I'll walk over there with you, but I ain't going in, this shit is fucking me up, I can't handle it, I'm about to go crazy or something T."

Trè took me to Sharod's room, nothing could prepare me for what I was about to see. Even though I'd been through this with Derek, seeing death will never be easy and it leaves many scars implanted inside of your psyche.

I saw my baby brother stretched out across the hospital bed. The tears poured out of my eyes as my face frowned up in despair, grief, shock and sadness. A few nurses were in the room trying to hold back tears after seeing my reaction. I put my hand on his head and began talking to him.

"Sharod, it's Tiara, your big sister, wake up please." I began shaking him, "Wake up, let's go home Sharod! Sharod, wake up please!!! You can't leave me, Sharod please wake up come on!"

His head still felt warm, I knew he was gone and that there was nothing that they could do to revive him but I demanded it. "He's still warm, my brother's head is still warm, can't y'all revive him? Somebody better do something in this bitch! Wake him up please!"

I held my little brother in my arms and looked at one of the nurses in her eyes as I pleaded, "Please save him, I want to take him home, please, he's my baby brother, he's only a baby, help him."

She swallowed hard as she tried to calm me down. "Ma'am, he's gone, we tried everything, I'm so sorry."

A tear snuck out of one of her eyes and she tried to wipe it quickly.

Trè heard me screaming from the hallway and came in the room to embrace me. It felt like our connection was broken, our bond was disabled. It would never be the same without me, Trè and Sharod, what were we going to do without our little soldier?

Trè began crying again. "It's on T, they took our brother, I'm going to make the niggas that did this hurt just like we do right now." His tears soaked my hair.

One of the nurses wheeled my mom into the room, Trè and I let go of each other to try to be there for her. She got up out of the wheel chair and went straight over to Sharod. "My young Prince, my young handsome Prince, you're at peace now." She began crying so hard that she couldn't catch her breath. She started rubbing his hands, his face and his long braids. "Be with God my baby, until we meet again, mommy will see you soon." She turned around to look at me and Trè, our eyes were red as apples. "Do you see what y'all did to my baby?" She raised her voice, "Do you see what y'all did!"

Trè and I looked at each other and I tried to speak. "Ma, we didn't do this, you can't blame us."

"Shut up!" she screamed. She walked over to Trè looking at him with an ice cold look on her face. "You were never a good example for him, you never showed him how to be a man. All you showed him was the street life. I kept telling you that he wasn't like you, now look at him!" She pointed to Sharod and then turned to me. "And you! Ms. Tiara, Miss I'm taking my brother out of the hood, you couldn't even take the hood out of you!" She stepped back and looked both Trè and I up and down. "I don't have anymore kids."

My heart fell out of my body and landed in front of my mom. "Ma, how could you put something like this on our conscience? Yeah I took Sharod out of the hood but I couldn't control his every move. He was his own person."

She closed her eyes and put her hand up. "I don't want to hear it! I blame the two of you for this and I'll never for as long as I live forgive you for this." She turned and blew a kiss to Sharod and she walked out. My mom's words were hurtful on top of losing Sharod, I never felt so shallow before in my life. I walked over to my baby brother and laid my head on his chest until the nurses made me leave. Before I left the hospital I cut off one of his braids and took it with me to keep forever.

I left the hospital that night losing two more people in my short life. I drove straight to Tony's, I don't know how I made it over his house because my eyes were flooded with tears and I could barely see the road. I needed Tony's comfort and I needed someone to tell me that what happened to Sharod wasn't my fault.

Flash backs of when Sharod first came home from the hospital when he was a newborn flashed in my mind and I began crying harder. My car was completely silent and all I heard was my screams and hard breaths from crying so hard. I started reminiscing about all the times that I took care of Sharod when my mom was too drunk to even acknowledge him.

All the blood, sweat and tears that I put into trying to make sure the hood wouldn't consume his life. To know that the streets had won that battle that I fought so hard to win trying to save my brother made me feel like a failure. I began thinking irrational and I even contemplated suicide. I quickly dismissed that thought because I couldn't take the coward's way out.

I tried to retain the strength that God gave me but I really didn't have anything in life to look forward to anymore. I lived more for Sharod than I did for myself, he was my everything, my all and now I had nothing.

I pulled up to the curb on the bottom of the hill and opened the door and started throwing up profusely. I felt extremely nauseous and every time that I would stop throwing up, I felt sick again and started puking all over the sidewalk. I saw a bunch of blue and white lights at the top of the hill in front of Tony's house when I started walking up the stairs and I ran to see what was going on. I saw Tony in cuffs with his torso bent over one of the police cars.

"Tony, baby what's going on?"

"Ma'am, can you step away from him, you can't be over there."

"T, just leave a'ight, that chick y'all fucked up called the jakes and they came and raided the crib."

What the fuck else could happen to me! My mom, my baby brother and now my man are not going to be in my life. I couldn't take another blow, I just felt like a feather in a wind storm. I put both my hands through my hair and squeezed real tight.

"Tony, can I bail you out? I need you right now, you can't leave me."

"They found all my money in the crib so I know I ain't getting bailed out any time soon."

The officer lifted Tony up by the back of his shirt and placed him into the police car. "T, I love you, promise me you'll wait for me!"

"I promise Tony."

"Look inside the glove compartment of your car, I'll be waiting for my answer, I love you and don't worry about me."

The police officer shut the door and I closed my eyes and just wished that someone could take me away to somewhere where I couldn't feel anymore pain.

I overheard one of the cops saying that they found a key of coke along with a large lump sum of money in Tony's home. I ran back down to my car to open up the glove compartment. I shuffled through some of Tony's papers until I found a little black box. I opened the box and burst out in tears as the beautiful diamond glistened off the street lights.

I sniffed and pushed it on my ring finger and spoke out loud to myself, "Yes, Tony, I'll marry you." I sat in the car for over an hour and cried my heart out. I had nowhere to go, no one to lean on and for the first time in my life, I was completely alone.

I wanted to find the bitch that snitched on Tony and fuck her up. I wanted to find whoever killed Sharod and take their lives as well. But I knew that nothing that I could do would bring Sharod back. I got startled as my cell phone rung. I looked on my Caller ID and noticed that it was Renée calling, I really didn't feel like speaking to her because I knew that she wanted to talk about Sharod and I didn't want to talk about him and get even more emotional than I already was. I finally decided to answer the phone after realizing that I would most likely have to move in with Renée in the projects.

"Hello?"

"Hey T. I'm so sorry about Sharod."

I didn't say anything I just stared at the steering wheel as she spoke.

"I know you don't need anything else on your plate right now, but I have to tell you this."

I let out a sigh. "Renée, nothing can compare to what I've endured today."

She took a deep breath. "Well, I'm watching the news right now and Trè and his boys are the topic."

I snapped out of my trance and suddenly became interested in what she had to say."

"What do you mean, what are they saying about him, is Trè okay?"

"Yeah he's okay, but he's going to be facing crazy time. They killed a lot of niggas."

I sat back in the chair of my car and closed my eyes. "Renée, I don't want to hear any more. Can I come over? I don't have anywhere else to go. Tony just got locked up, his crib is hot and you're all I have right now."

"T, you know you can always come here."

"A'ight, I'm on my way."

Renée met me outside and she welcomed me with open arms. Of all of my girls, she and I were the most distant, but we always stayed down for each other. As I embraced Renée, my eyes filled with tears again. "Renée, Sharod is gone, I tried Renée, you know I tried, it's not my fault he's gone Renée, I tried to save him!"

"T, look at me." She grabbed my face. "It's not your fault, don't ever think that it was."

We held each other and cried together. "T, you don't deserve this shit, you're a good person.

You're the realest person that I've ever known, I don't know why bullshit keeps happening to you. But I'm here for you, you know that."

I wiped my tears. "Renée, I need you to hold me down for a bit till I get on my feet. You think your mom will mind?"

"Nah, your welcomed over here, you already know that girl."

"I'm gonna find a job and save enough money to move out on my own."

"Don't worry about that right now T, let's go in the crib and we'll worry about all that future shit later."

We walked into Renée's apartment in the projects and it was the place that I would call my home until further notice.

Epilogue

I'm still currently residing with Renée. I found out that I was throwing up because I was pregnant with Tony's baby. We never used protection so I knew it was bound to happen so aborting my baby was no option. My mom ended up really writing me and Trè off and hasn't spoken to us since Sharod's funeral where I kissed her and told her that I loved her. Trè is facing fifteen years to life. He found out that the dude that killed Sharod was the friend that Sharod had pistol whipped from trying to steal out of my mom's purse. Trè and his boys made sure that they killed him and whoever he was with. The little nigga should've seen it coming. When Orlando found out about Sharod, he took the coward's way out and committed suicide. I guess the guilt of abandoning his child for years had caught up to him and he couldn't handle it. All of Trè's letters are sent back to him every time he tries to write my mom, she writes return to sender on them and never even opens them, but I try to visit him when I can.

Tony was sentenced to five years and he's very excited about our new bundle of joy. The police confiscated most of his money but I managed to find a few pounds of weed in the trunk of the car he gave me. Renée helped me pump most of it and it's been holding us down for a little while now. I'm still trying to use my community college education to get a good paying job but I haven't had any luck yet. I often tried not to let depression get the best of me and when I found myself about to soak in grief, I rubbed my belly and realized that I had another life that I had to worry about stressing.

As you can see, there is no happy ending to my story, I never made it out of the hood and I'm in the same position that I was in years ago but even worse.

A year has now passed and I had a beautiful, healthy baby girl. I named her Shayonna Sharod James. I cried in the hospital once I realized that my mom really wasn't coming to see her grandchild, but I'm starting to adjust to the fact that she doesn't want anything to do with me.

I'm still living with Renée planning to collect welfare for the time being. I'm on the waiting list for Section-8 and I'm hoping that I'm selected soon so that I can have my own space for my daughter's sake.

One day I was sitting outside on a bench in the middle of the projects staring at the braid that I had cut off of Sharod's hair and I smiled. I was in deep thought reminiscing of old times when we were all happy when I saw one of his friends walking up to me. "Excuse me, you're Sharod's sister right?"

I looked at the young thug. "Yeah."

"Sharod was a young legend, he was getting control of these streets like Trè and he had a lot of niggas fearing him. We were the same age but I looked up to him. I just wanted to let you know that we miss him and me and my niggas are out here living for him everyday."

A tear glazed one of my eyes as the young boy started walking away. "Hey!" I yelled out to him. The young boy turned around and I gripped Sharod's braid tight in my fist. "Make sure you keep repping for Sharod, keep his memory alive." My eyes filled with tears.

"Oh you already know!" He pointed at his shirt, it had a picture of Sharod on it and it read: "Rest in Peace, Young Rod, The Street's Prince." The smile on Sharod's face in the picture on his shirt motivated me to keep on keeping on for my daughter's sake. God took a life and gave me a new one and I'd be damned if I let my daughter suffer like I had to and I knew that Sharod wouldn't want me to just give up. I'm going to get on my feet and strive for a better life but for now, I'm just another chick in the hood with a story to tell.

But I promise, I won't give up.

ACKNOWLEDGEMENTS

First and foremost I would like to thank my father God in heaven, without him I wouldn't possess the ability to speak through my writing. I thank him for bringing me through many rough trials and tribulations; with him all things are possible.

To my two beautiful children Shyna and DeVandre; Mommy grinds hard for y'all and I will continue to do so until you are able to achieve your own dreams. You two complete me, you're my world and I would do anything for you. To Rahdahl, thank you for encouraging me to continue to reach for the stars and always reminding me that the sky is the limit. To my beautiful mom, Della Smith, thank you for riding this one out with me. Thanks for believing in my dreams and staying on me about not losing my focus. God may test us but eventually He always paints smiles on a face full of sorrow.

To my two brothers, Andre -aka- Dre (RIP) and Darryl. We've been through a lot together and our bond still remains strong although God called Dre home first. Andre, my little soldier, everything I do in this world, I do it for us. Losing you was the hardest thing that I've ever had to handle and I'm still struggling with it until this very day. I named my son after you and when I look at him I see you and it hurts that you never had the chance to meet him. But I'm inspired to keep reaching higher. We only live once and your short stay in this world has encouraged me to strive for more. You were truly

one of a kind and I will rep you until the day I leave
this earth. Darryl, big bro, my big homey, I love you
eternally. Boy have we been through some storms
but we made sure we kept God first so that's why
we are still here to fulfill God's purpose.
Our little brother accomplished what God sent him
here for and now it's our turn before he calls us
home. Stay up; you'll be home soon enough.

To my girls, The Dime Piece Collection, I love y'all
chicks like no other. Yeah we been through some
tough times but what group of friends hasn't? When
I first told y'all about my new literary career, y'all
had my back from day one and I love y'all for that.
I'm looking forward to many more years of
traveling and seeing the world with y'all. We grew
from little girls to grown ass women and I applaud
us all for that. My best friends Nichole and Kiyana;
thank y'all for listening and riding with me as I
grinded. Kenya and Toya my dogs for life, y'all
keep a chick grounded fo' real fo' real. Chanell, we
go back like four flats on a Cadillac, thanks for
believing in me. Precious, my homey and graphics
designer, girl you know your skills are taking you
places. To Lee from 337 photos, thanks for hooking
me up and always taking some fly ass photos. I
would like to thank Danyell from Hightower
Editorial Services, Life Changing Books and all of
my fans, family and friends that encouraged me and
supported me. I thank you all and I love you from
the bottom of my heart. This is a fiction novel
inspired by, but not based on my life. The events in
this book did not take place. I hope that you will

continue to enjoy more of my novels and anticipate reading "A Hood Chick's Story, Part 2." Coming soon!!!!

I always say, dreams do come true and I'm living proof.

GOD Bless,
LaShonda DeVaughn -aka- Shonda
my website
http://lashondadevaughn.page.tl/Home.htm